THE *Misadventures* OF
MAGGIE MAE

SERIES BOX SET BOOKS 1 - 3

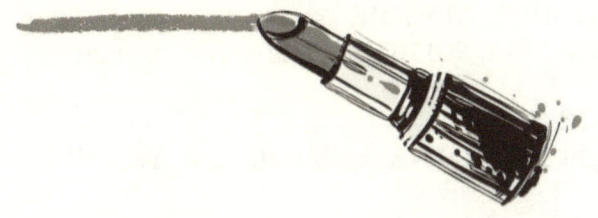

BETH
YARNALL

THE MISADVENTURES OF MAGGIE MAE
SERIES BOX SET BOOKS 1 – 3
Beth Yarnall

Cover Designs: Mayhem Cover Creations

BOOKS BY BETH YARNALL

Maggie Mae Misadventures
Wake Up, Maggie
You're Mine, Maggie
Find Me, Maggie

Pleasure at Home
Rush
Lush

Recovered Innocence
Vindicate
Atone
Reclaim

Gods of Redemption
Far From Honest
Far From Free
Far From Safe

Azalea March Mysteries
Dyed and Gone

Stand Alone Titles
A Deep and Dark December

Crafting Unputdownable Fiction
Making Description Work Hard For You
Going Deep Into Deep Point of View

THE *Misadventures* OF
MAGGIE MAE

SERIES BOX SET BOOKS 1 - 3

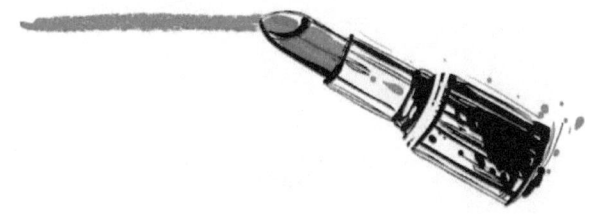

The Misadventures of Maggie Mae Boxed Set

Capture the hilarious antics of Maggie Mae Castro and FBI Special Agent Clive Poole in one special omnibus edition of The Misadventures of Maggie Mae.

Includes the first 3 books in the series:

Wake Up, Maggie

Maggie is the only witness to an Arizona state senator's death. Can Clive keep her safe and keep his hands off the hot body he's been charged to guard?

You're Mine, Maggie

Someone is sending Maggie strange anonymous gifts with the note You're Mine, Maggie. When her secret admirer proves his affection for Maggie by killing her coworker, Maggie and Clive work together to find a killer who will do anything to have Maggie. *Anything.*

Find Me, Maggie

Maggie's twin brother is missing and it's up to Maggie to find him. Maggie strikes a deal with the mob boss Miguel conned—if she brings Miguel back, her brother lives, if the man's henchmen get their hands on him first, all bets are off and Maggie could end up an only child.

THE MISADVENTURES OF MAGGIE MAE

Wake Up, MAGGIE

BETH YARNALL

WAKE UP, MAGGIE

Rearranging your cheating boyfriend's family jewels isn't a crime—unless your boyfriend is an Arizona state senator and he happens to have a bullet in his chest.

Caught at the scene of the crime, Maggie Mae Castro is the only suspect, and the only one who saw the senator's real killer—the skank ho he was cheating on her with.

FBI Special Agent Clive Poole has been shadowing the senator's every move for nearly a year. He's wanted Maggie from afar and knows she didn't kill the senator, but with temptation close enough to touch, it's now his job to protect her from danger.

Maggie finds herself falling for a man who knows everything about her from her juvie record to her shoe size. When she becomes the target of not one, but two killers, keeping Maggie safe is going to be more difficult for Clive than keeping his hands off the hot body he's been charged to guard.

Dedication

To *my* Super Agent, my husband, Mr. Y. for buying in to and supporting every single one of my crazy Lucy and Ethel schemes...including the one where I thought I could write a book.

And to my parents for being so strongly convicted politically that they've not only marched on our state's capitol but on Washington, D.C., as well. I'd bail you out—anytime, anywhere.

Wake Up, MAGGIE

THE MISADVENTURES OF MAGGIE MAE

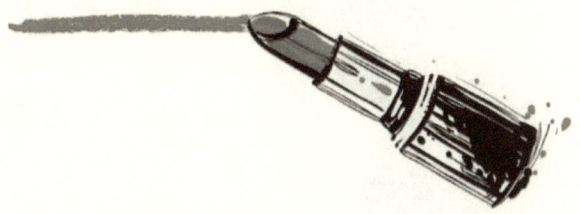

BETH YARNALL

Standing over Chuck Puckett's prone, naked body, sirens wailing in the background, I had done what I'd been dying to do for days—I kicked him square in the nuts. The pointy toe of my leopard-print, kitten-heeled pump had made a satisfying triangular dent. So satisfying that I kicked him twice more for good measure. The only thing I regretted about this later was the fact that the bastard was dead and didn't feel my sharp retribution.

Even hearing the words "Maggie Mae Castro, you're under arrest for murder", the taping of my perp walk—which had garnered over a hundred thousand hits on YourVid—being forced to wear a hideous orange jumpsuit after my clothes were confiscated as evidence, and being ditched by not one, but *three* public defenders, didn't ping on my shame-o-meter. Sitting across the cold metal table from my new attorney, explaining why I'd tried to rearrange Chuck Puckett's genitals while my lawyer defensively cupped his own, it suddenly dawned on me that I'd heard nothing about the skank ho Chuck Puckett had been banging behind my back.

"What about Crouching Slut, Hidden Man Stealer?" I asked.

Regis Dilton, AKA the attorney, who was dumb enough...or smart enough—time would tell—to take my case, glanced up from his notes to stare at me over the rim of his glasses. "What?"

"The slut Chuck Puckett was cheating on me with."

"The senator was cheating on you?"

Oh yes, Chuck Puckett was an Arizona state senator. But not just any senator—he was the conservative, Christian-family-values senator who'd tried and almost succeeded in passing legislation to have creationism taught in schools. The irony of him being found naked and dead, wearing lipstick and a long, blond wig, might have been funny but for the fact that I was now the accused murderess who, according to the morning paper, had desecrated their golden-boy senator in some sick sexual death ritual.

I filled in old Regis on finding Chuck Puckett in bed with his Asian sensation riding him like a prize bull and how she'd invited me to join them. I had declined the invitation of course, doing so with a lot of cursing and smashing...and maybe a little car keying. But when I got to the part where Chuck Puckett had lured me back to his mansion the following day with lots of pitiful pleading and how I'd shown up only to find the Jade Jezebel fleeing the scene of Chuck Puckett's murder, I faltered. I was pathetic. I had also been set up. Of this, I was sure.

Regis...not so much. "And you think this woman is the one who killed the senator, leaving you to take the fall. Do you have proof?"

"Well, it's not like I stopped to jot down her confession." If I had gotten a hold of her, I would've earned the murder rap honestly and could truly bask in the joy of getting to know old Regis here.

"Miss Castro, I suggest we stick to what we and the police can prove."

"What *can* they prove?"

He stacked his hands on the table. "They caught you in the act of desecrating the body of an Arizona state senator.

THE MISADVENTURES OF MAGGIE MAE

So there's that."

"That's all I did. And it wasn't desecrating, it was...anger management. I've been told I might have an issue in that regard."

"No kidding. You were also in possession of a firearm."

"Um, hello. We're in Arizona. Besides, it's registered."

"To you?"

"I didn't shoot him."

"Miss Castro—" he exhaled as though he was having a little anger-management problem himself, "—you were found at the scene of a murder, in possession of a firearm not registered to you, kicking the body of a beloved senator who'd been shot to death."

"Well, when you put it like that..."

There was a knock on the door. Detective Barry opened it. "We're releasing her. For now." He threw that last part in to scare me. It worked.

"I'm free to go?" I asked.

Regis was already stuffing his notebook in his briefcase like he had better places to be. I could hardly blame him. "Looks that way."

"And you were so pessimistic." I popped out of my seat. "Where are my things?"

Detective Barry tossed me a large manila envelope. I tore it open and peered inside. All it contained was the contents of my purse minus the gun. The purse itself was missing. It was my favorite one too. Chuck Puckett had given it to me for my birthday, not that I was sentimental or anything. But it was Prada, for jeepers' sake.

"Where's my purse? And jewelry?"

"The handbag is evidence. The jewelry is in a baggy at the bottom. Have a nice day." With that, the detective left like he'd done me some kind of favor. The bastard.

"I have an appointment across town," Regis said. "I'll call you." He dropped his business card on the table, making a quick exit as though he was the one who'd spent the night with Big Bertha and her prison pals and couldn't wait to get the jail stench off him.

I pulled out my cell phone and tried to turn it on. Dead. Great. How was I supposed to get home?

"Need a ride?"

I looked up into the dark eyes of a very large man in an ill-fitting suit who seemed to know not only who I was but the predicament I was in. I was already mentally undressing him and redressing him in something that would be worth stripping back off him. Too bad I could smell the cop on him.

"Yeah, no. That's okay. Is there a pay phone around here?"

"Down the hall, but you wouldn't want to use it without a hazmat suit." His voice rumbled through me like a commuter train making all the stops—Hot Guy City, Interested Town, and Turned-Onville. "Here." He held out a spiffy-looking phone that looked like it could control the space station. "Use mine."

"Would you mind switching it on? And setting it to 'phone'...you know, with the number-pad thingy?"

His lips kicked up at the corner, revealing a rather charming dimple. Damn it! I loved dimples on a guy.

"Sure. Here you go."

The tips of my fingers slid across his palm. There was a snap and I got a little jolt. Yeah, not sparks. Just plain old static electricity.

"It's...ah, dry in here I guess." I laughed, but it wasn't an aren't-I-witty chuckle, it was a crazy-psycho-lady kind of cackle. My flirting skills had been seriously ground to nubs by Chuck Puckett. I'd better shut up before someone decided I should be put on a psych hold.

He watched me with his dark eyes, assessing. Probably thought I'd pocket his phone. Who was this Duane The Rock Johnson lookalike? And why was he being so generous with his cell phone minutes?

I kept my eye on him—like that was a hardship—and dialed my friend Tabitha, thinking she might be home, but then I remembered it was Tuesday and she had rhombus...no zima...no, that wasn't right...she had some kind of dance-fitness thing so that was a no-go.

I handed tall, dark and disturbing his phone back. "How do I go back to the number part?"

"How about you tell me the number and I'll dial it for you?"

"Yeah, sure." I rattled off Xavier's number. Hot Cop punched it in and then handed me back his phone.

Hot Cop and I eyeballed each other while I waited for Xav to pick up. I got the feeling I'd seen him before, but couldn't place him. Maybe I'd seen him at the department store where I worked. He didn't look like someone who'd step foot in the cosmetics department unless he'd been dragged there by a girlfriend. And why I found the thought of him with a girlfriend so depressing was beyond me. I really needed to get out of this room before Hot Cop's pheromones caused my ovaries to explode like confetti cannons.

"Finally," I said when Xav answered.

"Maggs?" He squealed like he was the one who'd been given a cavity search. "I've always wanted to be someone's one phone call. Holy mole, Chiquita, you're famous. It's all over the Internet and TV. You're YourVid famous. A hundred and fourteen...no, a hundred and twenty-one thousand hits on your Walk of Shame. Great mug shot, by the way." That Xavier. He was nothing if not a big fat boost to my insecurities.

"Gee, thanks. Can you manage to pull yourself away from my humiliation long enough to give me a ride?" I told him where to pick me up, promising to fill him in on the stuff that wasn't already on the Internet.

I gave old Chocolate Eyes his phone back. "Thanks Mr.... Detective..."

"Special Agent."

Yeah, I could see the "special". "What? Was Super Agent already taken?"

I got the full-tilt, crinkly-eyed smile. "Special Agent Clive Poole...FBI."

*M*y time with Chuck Puckett hadn't been all bad. We'd had some good times, like the time he took me to that carnival and won a stuffed animal for me. It might have been a photo op set up by his people, but at the time, I didn't care. As he'd handed me the oversized elephant that now rested in peace at the dump after being drilled with a few hundred rounds from my semiautomatic, he'd done so with the crooked grin that had reeled me in from the start. Chuck Puckett had oozed charm, secreting good-natured humor and gentlemanly goodness through every pore.

Good. That was how I'd describe him. Genuinely nice. The voters had thought so too, reelecting him to a second term by a landslide. He'd been handsome, blond with the ruddy-cheeked ruggedness from a *Land's End* catalog. Some girls liked bad boys, some suits. Me? I had a weakness for flannel and guys who could make a snowman and a cup of hot cocoa.

No, he hadn't been all bad. It was these sentimental musings that had led me to be sitting in my car in front of the church where Chuck Puckett would be eulogized. The same church where generations of Pucketts had been baptized, married, and mourned. Chuck Puckett had talked about us being married here as though it were a certainty and not the consolation it apparently had been for banging his southeast slut on the side.

The mourners filed up the steps in twos and threes. I recognized a few political cronies, family members, and friends. This was the crowd I'd run with during the year Chuck Puckett and I had been together. I hadn't thought I'd fit in, but he'd paved the way so that even the snootiest political wife air-kissed me with the same enthusiasm as she would the first lady. It was nice that so many had shown up to honor him.

I flipped down the visor and opened the mirror to dab at unexpected tears. I didn't know why I was crying over Chuck Puckett. I was supposed to be mad at him, furious at the cheating rat bastard. But a new, surprising emotion had replaced my anger—regret.

I climbed out of my car and picked my way around the puddles left over from last night's rain. I knew better than to wear suede pumps, but they'd gone so perfectly with my outfit. Head down, I didn't see the mob until I was in the midst of it and then it was too late. Shouts of "Why'd you do it, Maggie?" and "Murdering Maggie!" drowned out the somber strains coming from inside the church. Reporters jostled me from all sides, and I would've fallen if a strong hand hadn't gripped my elbow, steadying me.

"I got you." Super Agent Poole put his arm around me and hustled me up the church steps and into an unoccupied antechamber off the main vestibule. He didn't release me. Instead he gripped both my shoulders and gave me a little shake. "Are you crazy? What in the hell are you doing here?"

Not the reunion I'd pictured. In my imaginings there'd been flattering words and smoldering looks. What I got was two hundred and fifty pounds of pissed-off G-man.

"You shouldn't be here."

"Why not?" I asked. Who was this guy to tell me what to do?

"The cops are already looking for a reason to charge you with murder. Showing up at the victim's funeral only helps their case."

"Oh." I hadn't thought of that. No wonder the sharks out front had circled and bumped me like it was feeding time.

"I can take you out the back way." He started to steer me to a door on the other side of the room.

Holding up a hand, I dug in my heels. "Wait."

"What?"

"Why are you here?"

"A senator was murdered."

That was as good an answer as any, I supposed. "What about you?"

He huffed out a breath. "What about me?"

"Do *you* think I killed him?"

"No."

His one-word exoneration left me a bit lightheaded. He was the first law-enforcement type I'd come across during this whole mess who hadn't mentally convicted me on sight, including my own attorney.

"Why?"

"Does that matter? We have to get you out of here."

"I just wanted to pay my respects. I kinda loved him. You know...before."

His mouth compressed into a grim line. "I'm sure you did. Can we go now?"

We started for the door but stopped at the sound of voices. Super Agent and I exchanged looks. He put his finger to his lips, drawing my attention to their kissable perfection. The doorknob turned. Gripping my arm, he pulled me through another door, this one a tiny closet. Two men came into the room where we'd just been, arguing.

Super Agent shifted, rubbing me in a most titillating way. Man, did he smell good, all woodsy and leathery, like he'd been hiking outdoors. I leaned in for a sniff and bumped my forehead on his chin. He slid a hand into my hair at the nape, holding me still. I suppressed a moan and the instinct to arch into the caress. This man barely touched me and my body lit up like the Fourth of July.

"I can't find her," said a man who sounded a lot like the thugs my brother used to hang out with, all ego, no smarts.

"What do you mean you can't find her?" a guy with a distinct Boston accent answered. "You weren't supposed to take your eyes off her."

"She slipped out when that loudmouth lost it and kicked the senator, ruining everything," Thug said.

He was talking about me! I made a move for the door, but Super Agent blocked me and pulled me tight against him, clamping his big hand over my mouth. I stilled, my brain caught between wanting to rub up against him like a cat in heat and head-butting him. It was a rather annoying predicament.

"She knows too much," Boston said, his voice tight and ugly. "Find her. I don't trust her. In the meantime Miss Castro will make the perfect patsy."

I struggled, which did more to arouse me than free me. Super Agent seemed to be having the same issue. He backed me up against the side of the closet, pinning me with his big body. My heart jackhammered in my chest, making it difficult to find air. The big, giant mitt over my mouth didn't help matters either.

"That'll cost extra," Thug said, obviously afraid of Boston.

"You're trying to charge me *more* for a botched job?" Boston's tone sent a shudder through me.

"Jesus, stop squirming," Super Agent whispered in my ear, giving me more shivers. My quickened breath blew hot over his fingers as he smoothed his thumb over the pulse in my neck to calm me. But it didn't work. This guy set off all my libidinous tendencies.

"Expenses. That's all," Thug tried to reason.

"Eat 'em."

Super Agent stiffened and I sucked in air at the distinct *click* of a gun being cocked.

"Or I'll give you something else less pleasant to eat," Boston finished.

"Yes, sir."

A door opened and closed. They were gone. Super Agent relaxed once more. Well, most of him did. A very impressive part of him still stood at attention.

"They killed him," I mumbled under Super Agent's hand.

He removed his hand. "What?"

"They killed Chuck Puckett. Go arrest them."

"I can't do that."

"Why not?"

"I don't know who *they* are. Did you get a look at them? 'Cause I didn't."

"What exactly does the I in FBI stand for?" I shot back.

"It's not as simple as that."

"Fan-flipping-tastic. The only possible lead to exonerate me just walked out the door."

"Are you all right?"

Half turned-on, half scared, I shook my head. None of this was right, including my very wrong thoughts about Super Agent.

He cradled my face in his hands. "I'll find them for you."

As much as I wanted to hand over this entire mess to someone way more qualified than me to find out what really happened, I had to ask. "Why?"

"You don't deserve this. Any of this."

In the history of right answers this had to be the rightest answer ever delivered. Somehow my arms had twined themselves around his neck and now he was bringing me closer or I was pulling him down. Either way, in the darkness, we kissed, and this time the jolt was not caused by static electricity.

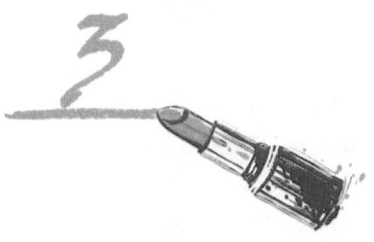

3

"Why do you call him Chuck Puckett instead of Chuck or Charles?"

Super Agent and I were sitting in a diner having a cup of coffee, looking like any couple on a date. Except this wasn't a date. And I couldn't help but feel as though I'd be struck by lightning at any moment for locking lips inside the church where Chuck Puckett was being mourned. Plus, I'd missed the funeral and was feeling sorry about it. For all his faults and failings, he hadn't deserved to be murdered.

"It was kind of a joke between us." I could feel my cheeks pinking. Talking about an ex-boyfriend with the guy I'd just swapped spit with wasn't my normal MO. If Chuck Puckett was ever going to haunt me, this would be the perfect time for him to make an appearance.

Super Agent nodded, the fluorescent lighting creating a halo around his cleanly shaven head. I didn't usually go for bald guys, but this one had macho to spare and there was a Zen-ness to him, a calm that seemed to quiet the rush inside of me. Who needed hair? Lord knew I had enough hair for the both of us, cascades of thick, black curly stuff that took forever to comb out.

"What should I call you?" I asked to change the subject.

His gaze drifted to the cup in front of him. "I think it's

probably best if you called me Agent Poole."

Wow. Where was Guinness when you needed them? This had to be a new land speed record for getting dumped. "Fine."

"Maggie—"

"Miss Castro. We may as well be consistent."

He finally had the balls to look at me. "I didn't mean for that to happen back there."

"You're not married, are you? Because that would just be the cherry on top of my giant, craptastic sundae."

He held up his bare left hand.

"Well, that's something, I guess."

"I'm sorry—"

"Don't. Okay?" I grabbed my purse. "Thanks for the protection, the fantastic make-out session, and the coffee. See you around."

As I walked past, Super Agent grabbed my wrist. "Sit down. Please."

"I don't need this. I've got enough going on with an angry mob of reporters, my sudden national notoriety, oh, and that other little thing...the murder rap hanging over my head."

"I need your help."

"Right."

"Sit down and let me explain."

I wanted to say no. I really did. But the look in his eyes stopped me. I sighed and slid in across from him, pinning him with the beady eye. "This better be good."

"What do you know about Trinh Pham?"

"You can get it with chicken or shrimp?"

"I'm serious."

"So am I. I have no idea what you're talking about."

He sat back and studied me. "She's the woman the senator was having ah...how can I put this delicately...relations with besides you."

"I have a paper cut you could pour lemon juice on. Why

don't we do that instead?"

"So you don't know anything about her."

"I know she was getting what I wasn't, riding my boyfriend like she was winning the Kentucky Derby. And that she's a screamer and her boobs are as big as your head. Also, she has a stupid tramp-stamp tattoo and wears too much makeup. That enough for you?"

"Wait a minute. What do you mean she was getting what you weren't?"

"I mean I saw more of Chuck Puckett bucking underneath her than I saw of him the whole year we were together. Including that time we went to the lake for some fun-in-the-photo-op sun. Look, I need to get home and feed my cat." I started to scoot out of the booth.

"You don't have a cat. Stop avoiding my questions."

I halted midslide and slowly turned back to him. "How do you know I don't have a cat?"

The reddening of his mocha-latte complexion might have charmed me had I not had the sudden feeling that an anvil was about to be dropped on my head.

"I've been watching you," he said, his words careful and testing.

"Watching me."

"You're my assignment."

"I'm your..." And then the anvil hit. "Well, isn't that stalkerific. I am so out of here." This time he didn't stop me. Tears burned behind my eyes, and I was so intent on putting him behind me that I didn't realize he'd followed me until I got to my car.

"Maggie, wait. Let me explain."

"Help! Rape!"

He clamped a hand over my mouth and backed me up against my car. "Don't do that. People are watching us," he whispered.

I blinked up at him with wide eyes. His explaining skills could use a lot of work. So now it wasn't just him watching me, but a whole passel of unseen stalker agents. What had I done and to whom to have this landslide of good fortune?

"We've had the senator under surveillance for months. At first, we thought you might be involved. I was assigned to monitor you. I know you didn't kill the senator because I was following you. You were home watching a movie until the senator called and invited you over. He was already dead when you got there."

I tried to talk around his hand. He really needed to stop muzzling me.

"Promise not to scream again?"

I nodded and he removed his hand.

My words came out in a rush of relief. I was saved. "You're my alibi. Tell the police. They'll listen to you." I was so giddy about having an alibi that the creep factor of kissing the guy assigned to shadow me took a few seconds to click in, then, "Oh...eww."

"What?"

"Back at the church when you ki—"

His annoying hand was back.

"Not here. People watching, remember?"

I glared up at him. He was in severe danger of losing a digit.

"Get in the car and I'll tell you everything."

*W*e were finally getting somewhere, but it sure wasn't any place I'd ever wanted to visit. Super Agent spun me a web of deceit, double agents, and doubling down. Gambling, that is. Apparently, Chuck Puckett had his fingers in more pies than a professional pie-eater. I sat and listened, all the while trying to reconcile what Super Agent was telling me with the Chuck Puckett I knew. His tale just didn't jibe...if you overlooked the Asian cowgirl thing.

"Are you sure we're talking about the same guy? Tall, blond, talked like Madonna? Wouldn't eat anything that grew underground or walked on two legs?"

"Of course."

"You're the super agent here; why would you need my help? It seems to me you've got almost everything figured out. Oh, except who really killed Chuck Puckett. It would be ever so nice if you could riddle that one out."

"Did he ever give you anything to hold for him?" he asked.

"You mean like a bag of money or the passwords to his offshore bank accounts? No."

"What about presents?"

"Just the obligatory Valentine's, birthday kind." Chuck Puckett bought me things all the time. Sometimes little things, sometimes big things, but nothing that sent up any flares for me.

"And you're sure you'd never seen Trinh Pham before? Maybe in the senator's office or home?"

"Keep saying her name and I'll do to you what I did to Chuck Puckett."

He clamped his legs together. "Sorry, it's just that you're the only one who's ever seen her."

"And more of her than I'd ever want to." My thoughts skidded to a halt and rewound. "What do you mean I'm the only one who's seen her? You know I don't have a cat and probably know what movie I was watching when Chuck Puckett called, but you don't have any surveillance footage of Slutzilla?"

Embarrassment tinged his cheeks again. I'd never thought a guy blushing could be so sexy, but Super Agent was making it work for me…big time.

"No. And you've seen her twice. That makes you an exception we think she'll want to rectify."

"Rectify as in…?" I made a slicing motion across my neck.

He nodded. "We don't know who she is or how she fits into the equation. Our best guess is she's a hired assassin who went rogue, but we're just not sure. We think she might not have known you'd be there the night she killed the senator."

"How do you know she killed Chuck Puckett? What about Thug and Boston?"

"Who?" He shook his head. "Never mind. You. You're a fairly reliable witness since we know you weren't involved in any of the senator's activities, and you told the police you'd seen her there. By the way, next time you're arrested, maintain your right to remain silent until your attorney arrives."

"You say that like you think there'll be a next time."

"This wasn't your first arrest."

I crossed my arms over my chest. "What *don't* you know about me?"

"I don't know why you put peanut butter and jelly on a bacon cheeseburger."

"Try it and you will."

"Not a chance. I'm a vegetarian."

His squinty-eyed grin did interesting things to the parts of me that Chuck Puckett had long left to gather dust. Under normal circumstances I would have been half in his lap by now, but even though we'd fogged the windows, the knowledge that other agents were out there watching us kept me firmly in my seat.

"Stop looking at me like that."

I blinked innocently up at him. "Like what?"

"Like I'm a bacon cheeseburger slathered in PB and J."

"I have no idea what you're talking about, *Agent Poole*."

"God, you have a smart mouth." His gaze dropped to my mouth.

My lips parted and my breathing sped up. His did too. The steamed-up car windows suddenly felt intimate, as though we were all alone in the world. He reached for me, grasping the back of my head, and pulled me to him. Our lips met on my low groan. This felt right, his body up against mine. It felt right and hot and oh, so intense, I thought I'd melt right there in a puddle of need and want. He made a deep-throated sound and bent me back to lie down.

All the years I'd had my old Pontiac, I'd never been so grateful for bench seats. I pulled Super Agent down on top of me. He was heavy in a really good way. It had been *so long* since I'd had a man on top of me. And he knew what he was doing, tracing my jaw with kisses, his hand creeping up under my shirt. Wrapping my arms around him, I brought him closer. He fit me so well I let out a purr of pleasure and wriggled closer, rubbing my pelvis against his.

He gripped my hip to still my movements and rose up

to look down at me. "Keep doing that and it'll be over before it starts."

"Are we starting something? 'Cause it feels started to me. In fact, I might already be halfway finished."

He grinned down at me, that cheese-eating grin I now associated with his being inordinately pleased with me. His gaze traced every inch of my face and I felt the longing mirrored in his expression. "You're so crazy beautiful." His words were barely audible, almost as though he was speaking to himself. "If I had you I wouldn't want anyone else."

No one had ever spoken to me like this. All I could do was stare up at him, completely dumbfounded.

"Do you think..." He cleared his throat. "Do you think we could put a bookmark here and come back later?"

"How much later?"

"Until we find Trinh Pham."

"I told you not to say that name." I pushed at him to get off me. Of all the things he could've said to me, that was the one thing guaranteed to douse my ardor. "Thanks for the cold shower."

He sat back slowly, watching me straighten myself as though I'd vanish or something. "My job is hard enough as it is."

I looked pointedly at his lap. "Not likely."

"You distract me. I can't get distracted."

"Seems to me you don't have a job anymore. You know I'm not a part of whatever it was Chuck Puckett was doing. You won't tell the police I didn't kill him, and I gave you all of the information I have on the Vietnamese Vixen. As far as I can tell your job here is done and maybe we should be too." I was bluffing...badly. I couldn't stop looking at him like he was a big ole giant bacon cheeseburger with peanut butter and jelly and I hadn't eaten in days. Years, even.

"That's the thing; my job with you isn't over."

"It's not?"

He shook his head. "My job now is to protect you, make sure nothing happens to you."

"Like a bodyguard?"

"Exactly like a bodyguard."

I would have made a crack about the ways in which I'd like him to guard my body, but reality locked the words in my throat. It wasn't enough that the tattooed tramp had banged then killed my boyfriend, leaving me to take the rap. I was now at the top of her hit list with nothing but Super Agent between me and death.

*W*hen Super Agent had first proposed his staying in my apartment to guard me, I readily agreed, swept away by visions of foreplay days and fornicating nights. Boy, had I been wrong. He stuck to his no-nookie rule like he'd been sworn to the priesthood by the pope himself. Just when I began to doubt his interest, I'd catch him looking at me as though he'd mentally stripped me and was cartographically tracing my every slope and curve.

It was those looks that kept me awake at night, wondering if I'd ever get to touch the tightly packed muscles I knew lurked beneath those horribly baggy suits. After I accidentally on purpose caught him coming out of the bathroom with nothing but a towel around his waist, he stayed dressed night and day. I was pretty sure he was showering in those damn suits now.

To make matters worse we hadn't heard a peep from the Mata Hari madam, and I was beginning to think Super Agent's theory of me being on her hit list was as farfetched as me losing the extra twenty pounds I'd been carrying since the day I was born.

"Can't I just go to the store and say hi to my friends?" I asked one bright and shining morning.

Super Agent glared at me over the top of his coffee cup.

"No."

"I can't afford to stay home from work another day."

"The press is still hounding you."

"Not as badly as they were before. Besides the store has security." My job as a beauty advisor for Estelle Landers Cosmetics wasn't as glamorous as a special agent for the FBI, but it paid the bills and kept me ankle-deep in beauty products.

He looked back down at his phone and made a "we'll see" noise. The majority of his speech had been reduced to noncommittal grunts and long-suffering sighs. I wanted to say it was my charm, but I was pretty sure it wasn't. Our forced confinement was getting to him too.

"I'll call my boss to let her know to put me back on the schedule." I pulled out my cell phone to make my call. "Next week we're having a gift with purchase, and I can't afford to miss the extra sales money."

"You'll have to explain me."

"Hopefully you'll be gone by then."

He raised his eyebrows at me.

Jeez. Such a Sensitive Sally. "You know what I meant."

He returned his attention to his phone, leaving me to stare at the top of his head. Conversation over. All morning he'd been texting and emailing his thumbs to bloody stumps. Something was afoot.

My phone rang, and a quick look at the display told me this was a call I needed to take in private. As I slipped off the barstool and padded down the hall, I could feel Super Agent's gaze on me. I'd never taken a call out of his presence and I could almost hear his gears spinning out questions three at a time. Two could play the I've-Got-a-Secret-Na-Na-Na-Na-Na Game.

I closed the door to my bedroom and went into the closet. "Hey, Jonas."

"Hey. Sorry it took me so long to get back to you."

"No worries. Were you able to find anything out?"

"I posted the image you gave me on a couple of forums and I think I may have found your guy. There's an artist out of Amsterdam who recognized the ink. I'll text you the deets."

"Thanks, Jonas. I owe you."

"When are you going to come in so I can finish you?"

Jonas still needed to fill in the color on my newest tattoo. "Probably next week."

"Text me and I'll fit you in. You know, now that you're not with the senator anymore, we could go out. Dinner or something. What do you say?"

"I say I'll text you next week."

"Why do I get the feeling you're not serious?"

I cut my gaze to the wall where Super Agent sat on the other side, stewing like an overfilled crockpot. "'Cause I'm not. Thanks again, Jonas. Bye."

I disconnected the call and sat down amongst my shoes, waiting for Jonas to text me "the deets". A couple of days ago Super Agent had put me in front of a sketch artist to get an idea of what Trinh the Trollop and her tattoo looked like. When he wasn't looking I snapped a pic of both sketches to do some sleuthing of my own. Why not? No one in this mess had more at stake than me.

A *bing* later I had the name and phone number of the shop that had possibly inked Tramparella's tattoo. Now all I had to do was figure out how to dial overseas.

Suddenly the bedroom door burst open. "What in the hell do—" Whoa. Super Agent sounded scary when he was pissed. I wouldn't want to be on the wrong end of that. "Maggie! Where are you?" Oopsie. Too late.

I slid the closet door open. He didn't sound half as scary as he looked. His chest was all puffed up, and his shoulders looked a mile wide. Now I knew why he wore such horribly baggy suits. It was like he'd grown two sizes, his anger filling in the gaps between the sags.

It took him a moment to find me amongst the dresses

and skirts. "Why are you in there?"

I held up my phone.

He offered me a hand up. I took it, fighting my way out of the closet one-handed. By the time I escaped, he was shaking his head and battling a smile. "You are the oddest woman I've ever met."

"I'll take that as a compliment."

"Don't." Uh-oh. Angry Agent was back. "I didn't see any harm in you sending that picture because I didn't think anything would come of it. But now... Stay out of this investigation. You have no idea who you're dealing with here."

I did a double take. What now? "You're listening in on my phone calls and reading my texts?"

"We thought it best in case Trin—"

I pointed my phone at him. "Say her name and you'll be gargling your balls for weeks. And who in the name of all that is private is 'we'?"

"You're not going to go out with that Jonas guy, are you?"

"What? That's the take-away from this cluster?"

"He's been convicted of aggravated assault. You shouldn't even have him as a friend, let alone go out with him."

"You're investigating my friends too?" My voice went supersonic, setting off car alarms and howling dogs.

"Well, yeah. It's my job."

"Your... You know what? You're fired!"

"You can't fire me."

"No?"

"No."

"I can kick your ass out of my house."

"Don't be ridiculous, Maggie."

"Miss Castro to you."

"We're back to that?"

I shot my arm out and nearly flung my phone. "Get

out."

"Fine. I'll be next door if you need me."

What the...? I propped my hands on my hips. "What do you mean, next door?"

"We rented the apartment next door."

"*We* again."

"I don't work alone. We set up a temporary command center."

Well, that explained Mr. Hands-to-himself I'd been living with. The walls in these old apartments were as thin as my patience with him at the moment.

"How many people do you work with?"

"Two or three, depending on what's happening."

"And they're doing what?"

"We've got eyes on every corner of this building. As well as tracking the latest info as it comes in."

"Inside my apartment too?"

"No. That's why I'm here."

I nodded.

He eyed me as if I were a coiled rattler. "What's going on inside your head?"

"Oohhh," I moaned loud enough to be heard through the wall, then whispered, "Nothing."

"Maggie..."

"Oohhh, yeessss!"

"Stop it."

"Don't stop!"

"You're pushing your luck."

"Oohhh, yeessss. *Harder!*"

He covered my mouth with his, and suddenly I was back to the wall, his knee wedged between my legs. I gripped his shoulders and met him kiss for kiss. I didn't remember wanting anyone or anything as badly as I wanted him. He broke the kiss long enough to pull my shirt over my head, then took a half step back and sucked in a breath. Exactly the reaction I'd hoped for when I'd put the purple lace bra on that morning on the off chance he'd finally break his vow of chastity.

"If you stop now," I warned, "I'll make good on my earlier threat."

"Not a chance."

*H*e took me hard and fast, right there up against the wall after we'd cranked up the TV and radio as cover. Thankfully it was an outside wall, or his friends next door might have thought we were having an earthquake. Angels sang. Fireworks went off. I might have even died briefly. All that pent-up sexual frustration was ten tons of dynamite packed tighter than a starlet in designer jeans.

One thing about Super Agent, he was incredibly thorough in his investigation techniques, leaving no spot on my body unexplored. The second time on the bed was where Super Agent really lived up to his nickname. I was pretty sure I saw God that time, and he whispered, "You're welcome."

We lay in the aftermath, sheets and clothes strewn all around. A fine sheen of sweat coated his body, highlighting the hills and lowlighting the valleys. He looked as though he'd been sculpted from fine stone. Whereas I looked like I'd been molded out of Play-Doh by an art-challenged toddler. My hair, unruly on most days, now lay in tangled ropes around us, but I hardly cared about any of that with the zing of multiple orgasms still jolting my system.

"You're not going out with that Jonas guy," Super Agent decreed, barely out of breath. I might have hated him a little for that except I couldn't muster the energy for it. Or anything else.

I rolled my head to the side to look at him. "Who?"

"Damn right."

I snorted a laugh.

"That was a good lead he gave you." He sounded reluctant to admit it.

"You think?"

"Maybe."

"Can I ask you a question?"

"You just did."

"How long have you had me under surveillance?"

He answered without hesitation. "Almost a year."

I hadn't expected that answer. It was much longer than I'd ever imagined. He'd seen me at my best *and* my worst. I considered all the things people did when they thought no one was watching. Except in my case someone had been watching and that someone was now lying gloriously naked beside me. Alarm bells jangled at the back of my brain. Unease crept cold over me, obliterating my warm afterglow.

He must have sensed my agitation. Rolling toward me, he studied my expression. "I hated seeing you with him. I knew what he was into, what he would drag you into. There were times…"

I waited him out. Not because I was anxious to hear what he had to say, but because I was just so stunned. I pulled the sheet up to cover myself, needing that barrier. I was overexposed. He knew everything about me, every detail of my life. I hadn't thought about that until this moment, not all the way.

He reached out to touch my cheek and I flinched. He frowned. "Maggie…I'm sorry. I wish we'd met the normal way."

"Normal. I don't think I'd recognize normal if it walked up and introduced itself."

He reached for me again, slower this time. I stayed

still, but his touch felt different somehow. "When this is all over I want to take you out on a real date."

I sat up, easing out of his reach, and fashioned the sheet so that only my head was uncovered. "Yeah, I think we might have jumped the shark here."

He leaned up on an elbow. "What exactly are you saying?"

I tried to look at him, but all I saw was how stupid and impulsive I'd been. I knew nothing about this guy, and he knew everything about me. If I lived a thousand years I'd never learn all of the things about him that he'd known about me for months now. I didn't have the staff, resources or access the FBI did.

I rose from the bed, gathering the sheet tight. "I think you should leave."

*A*lone in my apartment, I tried to watch a movie, then read a book, then twelve other things that didn't take my mind off Super Agent. In the end, I gathered up the spent condom wrappers, stripped the sheets from the bed, stuffed them in the hamper and had myself a good long cry in the shower.

Some people might have wondered why I'd stayed so long in my unusual relationship with Chuck Puckett. The thing was, it was easy. *He* was easy, predicable as sunrise. I was happy. Mostly. He treated me well, took me places, made me feel special. He was my best friend. I could tell him anything, and I never doubted myself with him. Well, not until *that* night anyway. The illusions it had shattered still dotted my life, like shards of broken glass.

Had I jumped so quickly into bed with Super Agent to make myself feel sexy and desirable again, or were my feelings for him real? I couldn't be sure. It was all so tangled and twisted.

A knock at my door startled me. I tossed the magazine I wasn't reading aside and went to the door. Super Agent looked small and ordinary through the peephole, nothing like he was in reality.

He knocked again. "Maggie. Let me in. I need to talk to you about something."

I hesitated, my hand hovering over the knob.

"Maggie, please. It's important."

I pulled open the door, and we stared at each other for a moment, neither really sure of where we stood or what effort to put forth.

"Can I come in?"

I stepped back and he slid past me into the room, giving me a wide berth. I closed the door but kept my hand on the doorknob.

"That tip from your friend paid off. We think we've found the real identity of the senator's killer."

He didn't say her name. I gave him points for that.

"I have a photo I want you to look at." That was when I noticed the manila envelope he was holding. "It's a little grainy." He slid out an eight-by-ten photo and extended it to me.

Hesitant and uncertain, I stepped closer and took the picture from him. Our gazes locked. I could tell he wanted to tell me something. He looked pointedly at the photo. Whatever he had to say would wait.

The image in the photograph was as confusing and unexpected as everything else that had happened to me over the past few weeks. "It's a man."

"Look closely."

I studied the features, the eyes, the nose, the mouth, the mole under his right eye. The mole. Bringing it closer, my nose nearly touching it, I went over the features again.

"Oh my god. Ohmygod, ohmygod, ohmygod, ohmygod." I dropped the photo and backed away from it, wrapping my arms tightly around myself.

Super Agent picked it up and slid it back into the envelope out of my sight. "His name is Thai Dinh, a Vietnamese national. He's been on our watch list for a couple of years. Professional hits, terrorist activities—you name it, he's had his hands in it."

"He had boobs."

"Those can be faked."

"They didn't look strapped on."

"Were you really studying his boobs that closely?"

He had a point. I'd been more focused on the fact that she…he…whatever had been riding Chuck Puckett than I'd been on whether or not all his parts had been real. A few of the puzzle pieces slid into place, forcing me to look at my life with Chuck Puckett as a whole. I'd been his beard. I'd been arm candy he could parade before voters saying: *Accept me. I'm just like you—white, straight, and electable.*

I was such an idiot.

"Maggie, look at me."

I tried, but he was all swimmy, blurring in and out.

Next thing I knew he had his arms around me, gathering me against him. "I'm so sorry. You don't deserve this. He was an asshole to do this to you."

"No, he wasn't. He just couldn't be who he really was."

And that was the thing. I didn't blame Chuck Puckett. I didn't hate him. I couldn't even muster a fraction of the anger I'd felt for him. He was the tragic figure here, not me. I felt sorry for him. Society had made him who he was. We'd dictated his life for him. He could have the only thing he ever wanted if he broke off a chunk of himself and lived with that gaping wound. He'd only ever wanted to serve. To do right. But he'd gone about it all wrong.

And I had to look at my part in all this. I'd wanted the illusion. I'd helped perpetuate it, ignoring the small voice at the back of my brain that told me something was rotten in Boyfriendville. All the parties, the glamour and status of being a senator's girlfriend, I'd wanted it, encouraged it. I was just as culpable as anyone else.

I wasn't crying for myself. I was crying for him. Finally grieving the loss of the man I knew and the man I wished I'd known.

"Do you think I could see his grave?" I asked.

"If you want."

I nodded. I'd missed his funeral and my chance to say goodbye to one of the best friends I'd ever had. I couldn't let him rest until I told him how very much I'd loved him. And how very, very sorry I was.

*W*e stood before the Puckett family vault in a half-walled courtyard lightly landscaped with shrubs and bushes. Elaborate wreaths flanked Chuck Puckett's temporary grave marker. He rested beside a cousin, an aunt, four uncles, three out of four of his grandparents and his sister. His parents would have been at his funeral along with his remaining brother. The Puckett family had known more than its share of heartache.

I traced a finger over his name and dates of birth and death. He wouldn't see his thirty-sixth birthday next month. I'd already started to plan a party for him when the whole thing had gone down. He liked German chocolate cake. Funny I should think of that now.

Super Agent stood off to the side, scanning the flat rows of graves dotted with mementoes and flowers. I wished I'd thought to bring something. Flowers or some kind of token to show that I'd been here, that he'd mattered to me. And then I remembered the keychain he'd gotten me on our trip to New York. It was a cheap thing from a souvenir shop with a picture of the Statue of Liberty. I pulled my keys out of my purse and worked on freeing it from the tangle.

With one last slide around, it finally popped free and flew out of my grasp. I shot forward to grab at it. Above my head, a chuck of stone exploded into pieces, pelting me. Suddenly, I was flat on the ground, a two-ton Super Agent on top of me.

"Stay down!" he ordered.

Like I had a choice with him crushing me. He barked out instructions to someone somewhere about a shooter. Our harsh breathing filled the silence that followed. I could feel the pounding of his heart on my back. It matched my own erratic rhythm. *Shooter.* Someone had tried to take a shot at me.

No more shots came. Super Agent asked for a status update. He must have gotten good news because he blew out a breath of relief.

"Jesus, God. Are you hit?"

I tried to take mental stock of my state, but my mind got stuck on *Shooter. Gun. Kill.*

"Maggie?"

"No. I don't think so."

He eased off and rolled me over, pushing at my clothes to check for bullet holes. He stopped and stared at the top of my head. "Your forehead."

I reached up to feel and my hand came away red. "I'm bleeding."

He examined the wound. "Do you have a tissue or something?"

"In my purse." I looked around and spied it up against the mausoleum. "Over there."

He got up to retrieve it and that's when I saw the keychain in the dirt next to me. Broken. I sat up and picked up the pieces.

"Here." He crouched down next to me and handed me my purse. "What's that?"

"What's left of my tribute."

"Your...are you sure you didn't hit your head?"

"I'm fine." Sort of. I glanced up at the chunk of stone missing from where Chuck Puckett's permanent nameplate would eventually go. "That could have been me."

Super Agent's mouth flattened into a bleak frown. "Yeah."

"Thai Dinh?"

"You can say his name?"

"Not saying his name would be running from what happened. I can't do that anymore."

He gave me a small smile and lifted a lock of hair away from my face. "Good for you."

"Did they catch him?"

"No."

"You're the freakin' FBI, for crying out loud. You know what brand of tampons I buy, but you let a murderer get away from you twice?"

"We'll get him." He was all defensive about it, as though I'd questioned his manhood or something.

I shoved what was left of the keychain in my pocket and got to my feet. A little shaky and lightheaded, I swayed, catching myself on the half wall.

Super Agent was at my side faster than you could say "murder attempt". "I think you should get checked out." He started to call for an ambulance.

"Don't. I'm fine. It's just the adrenaline." Mostly.

I spotted a figure jogging toward us and ducked back behind the wall.

"Come on up. It's just one of my guys."

He walked over and met the man. I could tell something was up by the way Super Agent kept looking back at me, his expression growing darker as the other man spoke. By the time he returned to me, he looked downright dangerous.

"We need to move you. Now." He took me by the elbow and hustled me to where we'd parked the car. The other FBI dude was gone.

"How'd he do that?"

"What?"

"Disappear like that?"

He bundled me into the car without answering. As we pulled away from the curb, an ominous feeling came over me, and I shuddered.

"That wasn't Thai Dinh who shot at me, was it?"

"No."

"Who was it?"

"We don't know. It seems there's a new player in the game."

I'd lived my whole life on the principle *I won't pee in your pool and you don't pee in mine.*

Somebody was not only pissing in my pool, they were defecating in it.

I couldn't go back to my apartment, because as Super Agent had put it—it had been compromised. *Compromised.* A stupid word with a double meaning, neither of which were of any use to me at the moment. So there I sat in an impersonal apartment somewhere "safe", surreptitiously listening in on Super Agent's cell phone conversation with his superior. So far I hadn't been very impressed by this other agent's superiority, as it was his foul-up that had landed me here.

Super Agent ended the call and let out a frustrated sigh. "They were able to salvage a few things from your apartment. The rest is a total loss."

Total loss as in *fire. Fire* as in *firebombed. Firebombed* as in *a total and complete screw-up.*

"Fantastic."

"Insurance should cover most of it."

"Yeah, if I had any."

He stared at me as if I'd broken out my rusty Greek. *"You don't have insurance?"*

"Oh, gee. Did we just stumble on the only thing you

didn't already know about me?"

He scrubbed his hands over his face. "Holy hell."

"Yup. My thoughts exactly." I opened my purse for my Furious Fuchsia lipstick, because what do you do when everything you own has been destroyed and you have two people out there who want to kill you? You freshen up, naturally.

"You amaze me."

I looked up from the mirror. "How so?"

"You've just been shot at, everything you own is gone, and you're sitting there touching up your face."

"If I'm going down, I'm going down with lipstick on."

He grinned at me, and I realized how long it had been since I'd seen that smile. There hadn't been a lot to get cheered up over lately. Seeing it now put a lump in my throat the size of my Pontiac.

"I'm so freakin' crazy about you."

All I could do was stare at him. Stupidly.

He held up a hand. "I don't expect you to respond. I just wanted you to know." He came over to me and kneeled down beside me. "Will you go out with me?"

"Like a date?"

"Yeah."

"I don't know. I'm sorry. I just...I don't know. Maybe."

His smile widened. "I'll take that maybe."

"You're a very odd fellow."

"This is a very odd situation."

I couldn't deny that. This whole thing couldn't get any stranger if a troupe of circus elephants suddenly traipsed through this crappy apartment with monkeys on their backs, juggling cats.

"What's the plan?" I asked.

"The plan is for you to get some rest while I do some work." He got up, kissed me on the cheek and went back to his computer on the rickety little dining table in the corner.

"It's the middle of the day."

"Watch a movie or something."

I dropped the lipstick back into my purse, and it suddenly occurred to me that everything I owned was either in this bag or parked at the curb across from my burned-out apartment. I blinked, expecting tears, but it seemed I was all out.

Instead, I turned on the TV and flipped through some channels. "There's no cable."

"Sorry."

I got up from the couch and wandered over to the window.

"Don't stand there," Super Agent said.

"What?"

"Get away from the window."

Oh, right. Don't make the killer's job easy. I moved to the little kitchenette that was part of the living room/dining area and started opening doors. Not much to look at. Not much to do. I leaned against the counter and crossed my arms. I could see the computer screen over Super Agent's left shoulder from this angle.

"Why are you looking at pictures of Quinn?" I asked.

Super Agent half spun around in his chair. "You know this guy?"

I walked over and looked at the screen as he clicked through some of the photos.

"Yeah. He worked on Chuck Puckett's reelection campaign. An assistant to the assistant or something. Why? What's he got to do with any of this?"

"That's what we've been trying to figure out. The background search on him came back with some inconsistencies. Our surveillance only picked him up a few times and yet his name came up a lot in the senator's correspondence. What do you know about him?"

"He came around more often in the last couple of weeks before Chuck Puckett was killed. His job was pretty much limited to being a glorified errand boy, as far as I could tell.

He'd drop off this or pick up that. Those guys always used the back door, never the front. I don't know. I didn't pay close attention to him or any of them. All that campaign strategy stuff bored me." I hitched a shoulder. "Mostly I just showed up looking gorgeous to attend his political events, shook some hands, drank some crappy champagne, and then he'd take me somewhere nice afterwards."

"Arm candy."

"Yeah, pretty much. I would have done more if he'd asked. He never asked."

"Do you know Quinn's last name?"

I thought for a moment. I hadn't been lying when I said I hadn't paid close attention to Chuck Puckett's business. He bought me a dress, I wore it. He told me who to schmooze and I schmoozed 'em. He pulled me in front of the camera with him and I smiled. It was the least I could do for him after all he'd done for me.

"Taylor. No, Trask. Oh! I got it. Boyd. Quinn Boyd."

"You went through the T's to get to Boyd?"

"My mind is a strange and wondrous place."

"No kidding. Can you tell me anything else about him? Maybe something about his background or something the senator might have said about him? Sometimes it's the smallest slip that trips up these guys."

"That's kinda it. Wait. There was this one time when I caught him in Chuck Puckett's home office going through his desk drawers. He claimed he was looking for a pen and paper to write a note. It didn't make much sense to me at the time, but I let it go. Chuck Puckett seemed to trust him so I did too."

"Did you ever see him use the senator's computer?" he asked.

"Once, but Chuck Puckett was with him. They were working on something. Don't ask me what. They'd been holed up in his office for a couple of hours. I went in to prod Chuck Puckett to eat something. He'd get busy and forget sometimes. He was diabetic, so eating was important. And I have no idea why I told you that last part."

"You took care of him."

"Someone had to. Anyway, they spent a lot of time together in those last few days, and it struck me as odd at the time. Quinn was just a flunky, but Chuck Puckett treated him as though he was absolutely vital to the campaign."

"Hmm."

"What does that 'hmm' mean? You know more than you're telling me, don't you?"

"You'll probably find out eventually."

"Find what out?"

"The senator and Julius Clemmons, AKA Quinn Boyd, were having an affair."

10

"Who wasn't Chuck Puckett screwing?" I asked. "Oh, wait...me."

"Maggie..."

"I don't even think you could call it betraying, could you? I mean there would've had to be something *to* betray. Some faithfulness for there to be unfaithfulness. Some one-timing for there to be two-timing. Well, I guess there was some one-timing...all on my part. I went through more batteries... Anyway, yeah. Another affair. Got it. How does Quinn boinking my boyfriend fit into the picture?"

"He was a jerk to do that to you."

"I'm not mad at him. Mostly. I'm mad at myself."

Super Agent reached up and touched my cheek. I leaned in to the caress. It felt good to be touched. To have a guy interested in me for something more than my photogenic-ness and my ability to charm political snakes.

"Don't be. He should've been honest with you." He pulled a chair over for me. "Come and sit down."

"More bad news? Don't tell me...you and Chuck Puckett?"

"God, no. It's pretty clear where my interests lie." He winked at me, then cleared his throat back-to-business-like. "I've been considering why someone would go to all the trouble of torching your apartment. I want you to think hard." He pushed a piece of paper and pen toward me. "Write down everything the senator ever gave you, no matter how incidental."

"Why?"

"I have a feeling someone doesn't want whatever it is found."

"So they destroyed my entire apartment?"

"Exactly."

"Isn't that rather like killing the dog to get rid of the fleas?"

"They must want to get rid of whatever it is very badly. Yes. I can't come up with another reason why they'd destroy your apartment."

I got to work on my list while he went back to clickety-clacking at his computer. Thinking back to when Chuck Puckett and I first met brought back some nice memories. He'd walked up to the Estelle Landers counter just as I was pulling my purse out of the drawer to go to lunch. Normally I didn't let anything get between me and a meal, but he had the most amazing blue eyes, crystalline looking, almost like glass. I'd dropped my purse as if it held a nest of spiders and shouldered my coworker out of the way.

By the time I rang up the perfume he'd bought for his mother, I'd worked my wiles on him. He asked for my number. I gave it. And for the next year, my life was filled with beautiful places, not-so-beautiful faces, and never-ending political races. And I wouldn't have changed a day.

I jotted down all of the clothes, jewelry, shoes, and other trinkets Chuck Puckett had bought me during our year together. He'd had fantastic taste. The list was going to be longer than I thought. Sadly, they were all ashes now. I was on my second page when there was a knock at the door.

Super Agent produced a wicked-looking gun from out of nowhere and went to the door. Whoever was on the other side must not have been an assassin, because he opened the door, had a brief conversation, then closed it again. He came back with a paper grocery bag and sat it on the table.

"This is what we could salvage from your apartment. Any of it come from the senator?"

I stood up and peeked inside. It smelled like my three-pack-a-day Aunt Esther's old romance novels. The items were completely random and from different rooms of my apartment—a Christmas ornament, a mug, a photo in a frame of my brother and me at our graduation, a troll doll and a pair of emerald-green satin heels that Chuck Puckett had bought me to wear to some gala. I mourned the dress they'd matched; it had been a work of art.

And that was it. Everything I owned reduced to a stinky grocery sack.

"The shoes," I told him.

Super Agent took them from me and went to the kitchenette. A series of bangs and curse words ensued.

"What are you doing?"

"Examining the shoes. Did you finish your list?"

"Almost."

"Finish it."

I sat back down, worried about my shoes. Something pinched. I dug into my pocket and pulled out the broken keychain. Huh.

"Um, Mr. Super Agent?"

He turned to me with a half-torn-apart shoe in his hand. "Yeah?"

I sucked in a shocked breath. "What have you done to my shoes? My beautiful shoes?"

"Sorry." He had the good sense to look ashamed. "They might've had a clue inside."

"I can assure you they don't."

"How can you be so sure?"

"Because I think I've got what everyone's been looking for right here."

I held out one of the broken pieces in my palm to show

him. He took my hand and brought it up for a closer look.

"Well, I'll be damned. That's clever," he said.

"What is it?"

"A microchip. Congratulations. You found what everyone's been looking for."

*A*t some point, unbeknownst to me, Chuck Puckett had switched the original keychain he'd given me for an identical one with the hidden microchip. Handy things, microchips. As I found out, you can store information people would kill your ex-girlfriend for and firebomb her apartment over. Things like bank codes and safe deposit box information. A safe deposit box with evidence that Quinn/Julius had been accepting bribes in Chuck Puckett's name.

"Bribes for what?" I asked Super Agent.

We were on night four of being stuck in this crappy apartment together, which was starting to feel more like a hamster cage without the wheel. And I was either getting a contact high off all the cheap Chinese plastic furniture in this place or somehow, some way, Super Agent was growing on me. Like drawing-our-initials-in-hearts, scribbling-my-first-name-with-his-last-name, imagining-our-children kind of growing on me.

"An online gambling scheme," Super Agent answered between phone calls to and from his fellow agents. "Julius Clemmons used the senator to cover up an elaborate online gambling ring. If it were ever discovered, everything would've come back to the senator. From what we can gather, the senator found out what Clemmons was up to and tried to put a stop to it. That's when their relationship went south and Clemmons hired Thai Dinh to get close to the senator. He needed someone on the inside to plant more evidence and control the senator. Except the senator caught on again. We think that's why Dinh killed him."

"Why didn't Chuck Puckett just go to the authorities?"

"We think he was planning to but got killed before he could."

"So what you said before about Chuck Puckett being involved in gambling and all, that stuff was a ruse?"

He nodded. "A very elaborate one, yes."

"It sounds like you've got it all figured out. So go arrest Quinn so I can get out of this crappy apartment and back to my life."

"We're not sure where he is."

"We're back to that? Really?"

"If we could find anyone anywhere, there wouldn't be an FBI's most-wanted list, would there?"

He had a point. A very frustrating, infuriating point, but a point nonetheless.

"What's the plan then? Please tell me there's a plan," I said.

"There's a plan. Of sorts."

"If it's anything like the plan that got me shot at and my house torched, then I think you need to replace your planning committee."

"I'm on the—" He let out a frustrated sound. "The FBI is not the garden club. We don't have committees."

"So what's your sort-of plan?"

"I can't tell you."

"Why not?" I looked around the thrift-store-furnished shoebox I was temporarily calling home. "Who am I going to tell?"

"It's not a matter of you telling anyone."

"I found the microchip," I grumbled. "You'd think that would earn me a hint."

"I'm sorry. I can't. But I did get you cable," he offered.

"HBO?"

"No. But you have more channels than just the local ones now."

"Thank you."

"You're welcome." He went back to staring at his computer screen.

All this confinement was doing weird things to my judgment and perception. So was everything about Super Agent, from his scent to the way he said *crick* instead of *creek*. The other day he'd asked about laundry and added an R to *wash*. I'd nearly jumped him. And right now, the way the computer made his skin glow was having a peculiar effect on my underused libido.

"I'm bored. Let's have sex."

His head jerked up. "As tempting as that offer is...and you have no idea...I know you're not really serious."

"I might be half serious."

"I'd rather you be completely serious."

"Have it your way." I got up from the couch. "I'll just be in the bedroom...you know, going it alone."

A vein along his jaw throbbed and he stared at me as though he was rethinking his entire moral philosophy. I closed the bedroom door, feeling slightly guilty and a little turned-on. Yup, he was definitely growing on me, and I couldn't help but think that maybe that wasn't such a bad thing after all.

I woke up freezing, to the sound of rain through the open window and a gun pointed between my eyes. Thai Dinh stood over me, his pretty face half lit by the streetlight that beamed into the room every night as though we were being invaded by aliens. I opened my mouth, but my lungs seized and no sound came out. I'd always imagined how I'd react in a situation like this, and lying there in a frozen lump of fear wasn't it.

"Scream and I'll drop you right here." His lightly accented voice was unusually high-pitched but aggressive, like Mickey Mouse with a grudge to settle.

He produced a gag that smelled like feet, stuffed it in my mouth and strapped it around my head. He made me roll over so he could bind my hands behind my back. His motions were quick and efficient as though he tied people up everyday. Maybe he did. I shuddered at the thought.

All I could think about was how had he gotten in? This place was supposed to be secure. I was supposed to be safe. And where the hell was Super Agent and the mother-lovin' FBI?

He yanked on my arm. "Get up."

I complied. What else could I do?

He pushed me toward the door that led to the living room. I dug in my heels. Super Agent was asleep on the other side. He wouldn't know what was happening until it was too late.

"Get moving!" Dinh whispered, sounding like an angry balloon with a slow leak.

I shook my head. He was going to have to shoot me here. Super Agent would come in, guns blazing, at the sound. I might be dead, but at least he'd be all right.

Dinh leaned his bony frame into my back. "Move it!"

The thing was, I weighed more than he did. I was taller too. His pushing me was like a child trying to move my Pontiac. It wasn't going to happen.

I shook my head again.

"I should just shoot you here."

I nodded.

A befuddled frown settled between his brows. "You want me to shoot you?"

I swiveled my head back and forth.

"Then get a move on." He gave me another shove.

"Mmm."

"What?"

"Mmm mm mm mhh m mm mhh."

"I can't understand you." He nudged me again. "Let's go."

I shook my head and stomped my foot. Or really, his foot. He bent forward and I turned to apologize and accidentally clocked him under the jaw. He dropped like a sack of wet sand at my feet, the gun clattering against the cheap linoleum floor.

I stared down at him for a second, then my common sense finally decided to make an appearance, and I started kicking at the closed bedroom door. Super Agent burst into the room, sending me backwards. My legs caught on the edge of the bed, and I sat down, nearly tipping over sideways.

"What the—" Super Agent flipped the light on and took in the scene. He pointed his gun at Thai Dinh. "You did this?"

I nodded. "Mmm mhh mm mmm mhhh!"

He bent down and checked Dinh's pulse, then lifted Dinh's eyelid and blew on it. Nothing. "He's out." Super Agent glanced up at me. "Are you all right?"

I bobbed my head again. "Mmm mh mm."

"Hold on." He disappeared and came right back with a pair of handcuffs. He locked them around Dinh's wrists, then patted him down. He pulled out his cell phone and called the other agents.

"Mh mm mmm mm mmh mmmmh mm mh?" I showed him my tied-up hands.

"Oh, sorry."

He went to work on my hands, then my gag. When I was finally free, I launched myself at him.

"He-came-into-the-room-pointed-a-gun-at-me-tied-me-up-threatened-to-kill-me-all-I-could-think-was-that-you-were-in-the-next-room-and-that—"

"Hey, take it easy." He gave me a hard hug, then pushed me back to look at me, smoothing the hair back from my face. "You're all right. I've got you now."

I sucked in some air, huge gulps of it. Then I spotted Thai Dinh just coming around. Anger roared through me, and all I could think was that he'd killed Chuck Puckett. I shoved out of Super Agent's embrace, marched over to Thai Dinh, and kicked him square in the nuts. He jerked, curling over, but I wasn't done. I got in one more kick before Super Agent grabbed me around the waist and hauled me back.

"That's enough."

I struggled, all arms and legs, flailing like a two-year-old at a toy store. "Let me...at...him..."

"He's disarmed and handcuffed. How is that a fair fight?"

"How fair of a fight did Chuck Puckett get?" I countered.

"I let you get in that second kick for me for tying you

up, but I can't let you beat the hell out of him. That'd be very hard to explain."

I shook him off. "Fine."

He looked down at the man who'd caused so much heartache, then back up at me. "This is better than the plan we'd come up with."

"Hell, yeah. One down, one to go. And I think I know just how to get him."

*T*he thing about plans is that they never go according to plan. The FBI finally came through and used their superpowers for good the old-fashioned way...they tracked Quinn, AKA Julius Clemmons, through Thai Dinh's cell phone. He'd been holed up with Thug from Chuck Puckett's funeral, AKA Garvis Beets, in a swanky hotel on some unsuspecting person's credit card. Quinn had been waiting for Dinh to contact him to tell him that he'd completed the job. The wuss.

Turns out Super Agent and I had overheard Quinn arguing with Beets at Chuck Puckett's funeral. On the rare occasion I'd actually spoken to Quinn, he didn't have an accent. The sneaky, fake bastard. If it hadn't been for that damn on-again off-again Boston accent I might've recognized his voice and the whole sordid business of me being shot at, my apartment being burned, and my near abduction, would've been avoided.

I had begged Super Agent for two minutes alone with Quinn. All of this was Quinn's fault. Super Agent had twisted sideways, instinctually protecting his family jewels and told me in no uncertain terms, "No."

We were finally alone in one of those hotel rooms with kitchenettes in downtown Scottsdale that would be my home until I could find other, less-blackened accommodations.

"You can stay here as long as you need to," Super Agent told me. "Until you're back on your feet."

"Thanks. I guess. I'm not really sure how long that will be. I have some savings, enough to cover the deposit on a new place but not enough to replace everything I lost."

"There was a reward on an old case involving Thai Dinh. About 50K. I can see if I can get it expedited for you. You earned it."

"Hot damn. I won't have to borrow my brother's DNA-filled futon from college."

"I did what I could, but you might have to face the reduced charge of disturbing a crime scene. For, ah, kicking the senator."

"I'll deal with it. Can I ask you a favor?"

He shrugged. "Sure."

"Can you make sure that the press doesn't get wind of Chuck Puckett's...you know...proclivities?"

"That's important to you?"

"Yes. I feel like I owe him. I got so much wrong with him. I want to try and put things right somehow."

"I'll do what I can."

He shifted back and forth, jingling his pockets. He was nervous. That was so not like him. But then I was nervous too. The time had come to say goodbye. There was no reason to spend any more time together...unless we wanted to.

"I have something for you," he said, reaching into the satchel he'd brought with him from the car.

I don't know what I was expecting, but the fat accordion file he plopped down in front of me was not even close.

"It's a copy of my FBI personnel file. Everything you'd ever need to know about me is in there. I'm not even supposed to have it. I pulled in a favor from a friend. It's classified, so you should burn it when you're done." He nudged it toward me.

I touched a finger to it, tracing invisible circles over its blandness. He already knew everything there was to know about me. If I read this file, there'd be nothing left for me to learn about him. We'd be even.

He laid down his business card on the table next to the file with some extra phone numbers and email addresses scrawled on it. "Here's my contact info. All of it. My home address is in the file."

I didn't know what to say.

"Will you go out with me this Friday night?" he asked. "There's a new restaurant off Main that serves cheeseburgers twenty-three different ways, including a bacon cheeseburger with peanut butter and jelly. I checked."

I looked up at him and I knew there was no way I could walk away from what he was offering. Cheeseburger or no.

"I'll go out with you on one condition."

"What's that?"

I handed the file back. "Burn this yourself."

THE MISADVENTURES OF MAGGIE MAE

You're Mine,
MAGGIE

BETH
YARNALL

YOU'RE MINE, MAGGIE

Maggie Mae Castro is sure she's either losing her mind or she's fallen in love. She's not sure which would be worse. Lately she can't find anything, not her lipstick nor her grandma's pill case. All she wants is an aspirin and the ability to fire Shasta, the most useless beauty consultant to ever breathe air.

When Shasta winds up dead, crushed by steel shelves full of Shy Kitty cosmetics, Maggie doesn't believe it's an accident. Things get even stranger when anonymous gifts arrive, each with the same message: "You're mine, Maggie."

FBI Special Agent Clive Poole doesn't like strange men sending his girlfriend flowers and presents. He especially doesn't like the possibility that the creep might also be responsible for Shasta's death. He's sticking to Maggie day and night. Maggie is his *and only his*.

Maggie isn't thrilled about this, especially since their last full-frontal encounter ended with her dropping her reservations *and* her panties. But Clive will stop at nothing to keep Maggie safe from a madman who would do anything to have her.
Anything.

Dedication

To *my* Super Agent, my husband, Mr. Y. for buying in to and supporting every single one of my crazy Lucy and Ethel schemes...including the one where I thought I could write a book.

And to my editor, Jennifer Miller, for falling in love with Maggie's crazy and Clive's dry wit every bit as much as I have. I hope we have many more misadventures together.

You're Mine, MAGGIE

THE MISADVENTURES OF MAGGIE MAE

BETH YARNALL

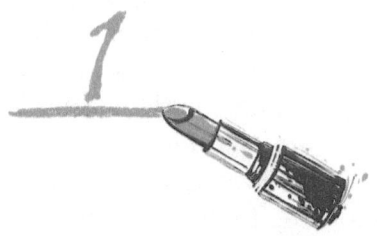

"*R*emind me again why I can't help her do a face plant into the tester unit?"

"Now, Maggie, you know Stratford's Department Store is a harassment-free workplace," Daryl Jenks, the cosmetics department manager, reminded me as he smoothed back the wispy hairs of his comb-over. He was in blue today because it was Monday—blue slacks, shirt, and sweater vest. If I ever forgot what day of the week it was, all I had to do was check to see what color Daryl was wearing.

We were watching the newest beauty consultant for Estelle Landers Cosmetics, Shasta Devereaux—don't even get me started on what a stupid name that was—use the counter tester unit as her own private vanity. She alternated between squealing into her cell phone at one of her inane friends about some party they'd attended last night and dipping her fingers into the powders and creams and smearing them on her face.

"You can't tell me that out of all the applicants she was the most qualified. She can't complete a sentence that doesn't have a thousand *like*s in it and doesn't end in a question. And look at her—" I gestured toward Shasta, who was now spraying herself head to toe with a perfume tester, "—she looks like she just rolled out of bed after an all-night party. Not exactly Estelle Landers beauty consultant material."

Daryl reached up and hesitantly patted me on the shoulder. "I'm sure you can teach her." He did a sliding step toward his office. "I'm counting on you to bring her around." I gave him a death glare, and he clutched his clipboard tighter, slinking closer to safety. "If anyone can do it, you can." He was in his doorway now.

"I'm not even going to disinfect that tester unit before I shove it sideways up your—"

"Harassment-free workplace!" *Bam!* He closed the door before I could fully deploy my threat. The rat bastard.

As counter manager I was Shasta's immediate supervisor, so it was up to me to bring frat girl up to Estelle Landers standards. I had half an hour before the store opened to wipe some of that black crap off her eyes and get her looking more like a human and less like a zombie. If I could get her face out of her phone.

I'd sat in on all of the interviews for a new beauty consultant...all except Shasta's. I narrowed my eyes at Daryl's closed door. He was so going to pay for doing this to me.

"She looks like you about seven years ago. Except you had a better rack," Xavier, my friend and Shy Kitty Cosmetics beauty consultant, said, his gaze dropping to my chest. He leaned across the counter as if he needed a closer look. "Still do."

"Gee, thanks. I'll hug that to me late tonight while I'm trying to sleep off the drunk caused by Lindsay Lohan over there. What the hell was Daryl thinking hiring her?"

He shrugged. "Better you than me, *chica*."

"If Skankarella makes me late for my date tonight, I'm going to have Clive put Daryl on the No Fly List." Clive as in Clive Poole, Special Agent for the FBI. A.k.a. Super Agent, my boyfriend and all-around hot-assed badass.

Xavier glanced over at Shasta who had her ear buds in

and was grooving to something that made her bend over and grind her ass against the life-sized cardboard cutout of Estelle Landers herself. "Twenty bucks says she goes to lunch and doesn't come back, and then shows up late tomorrow like nothing happened."

"If only I was that lucky. The problem is we start our gift with purchase tomorrow. We really need the help. If Shasta—" I couldn't help but roll my eyes every time I said her name, "—doesn't get it together, I'm putting Daryl in an Estelle Landers uniform and making him work the counter in her place." His pear-shaped body would look ri-di-culous in the navy pinstriped A-line dress all E.L. beauty consultants had to wear.

Xavier chuckled, his amazing mouth forming the smile that got women to open their wallets, making him the highest seller in the department. "I'd pay money to see that."

"See what?" Lance sidled up next to Xavier's counter and leaned an elbow on the backrest of a barstool like he was posing for an ad of the men's fragrance, Gent, which he represented at the perfume bar. He was always butting in between Xavier and me. I couldn't tell if his interest was in Xav or me. Either way, he was barking up the wrong tree. Xavier didn't do guys and I didn't do poser, loser assholes.

"Daryl in an Estelle Landers uniform," Xav answered, giving me a wink.

"Ha! Too right." Honestly, Lance's British accent was faker than Shasta's job qualifications. "Wouldn't that be a sight?"

Tabitha, counter manager for Enchanté Cosmetics and my best friend, joined our group. "Who's the Maggie lookalike? And why is she trying to eat a makeup sponge?"

"Oh, jeez. I gotta go. If she chokes, Daryl's going to make me take that management training class again. Fill her in, will you, Xav?"

Their laughter followed me as I made my way toward

the twit who did look a depressingly lot like me. I snatched the bitten sponge out of her fingers and held my hand out, palm up.

"Spit it out before you choke and I have to decide whether or not to give you the Heimlich before I've had my coffee. The odds wouldn't be in your favor."

She gave me a funny look, then spat out the chewed bits of sponge along with a big wad of saliva. Gross. I grabbed a tissue and wiped my hand, then pumped out a bunch of hand sanitizer. Who knew what diseases this girl carried? She was like a two-year-old.

"I thought it was like, you know, candy?" Her voice was as high as she was. If her pupils were any wider, her eyes would be as black as her hair.

I sighed. It was amazing this girl had made it this far in life with natural selection breathing down so hard on her. "There's nothing edible here." She kicked her head to the side, her eyebrows pinching together. "Nothing here is food," I clarified. "No eating. No using the makeup and perfume testers. They're for the customers. No talking on the phone. No ear buds." I pointed to the cardboard cutout of Estelle Landers. "No grinding, twerking or otherwise molesting the founder of Estelle Landers Cosmetics."

She nodded slowly, absorbing the rules I'd laid down. God, she really did remind me of myself at eighteen. If I could go back in time, I'd punch myself in the face and make sure know-it-all me didn't hook up with the tattooed idiot I thought was gonna change my world.

He had. And I had the rap sheet and tats to prove it.

"But I can, like, text?"

"When you're on break or lunch."

"So, like, when's my break?"

"Ten thirty."

"That's like two hours from now?" she whined. Everything was a freaking question with her.

"Try to hold up. In the meantime—" I handed her a wad

of tissues, "—find your eyes under all that kohl liner. It's called the smoky eye, not the charred-beyond-all-human-recognition eye. Also put your hair up, back, shave it off or whatever, but you're going to have to make it comply with Estelle Landers standards. That means it needs to be out of your face. You got the dress code booklet, right? It's all in there. Make it happen in the next twenty minutes and be ready to work when the store opens."

She gave me a long-suffering sigh/eye-roll combo that had me clenching my hands into fists. Great. This girl was going to seriously mess with my ability to stay on probation.

*W*here were my drugs? No, seriously. *Where were they?* I rifled through my purse again, looking for the antique pill case my grandma had given me, and the precious aspirin inside. Gone. I'd been misplacing a lot of things lately. Tabitha teased that it was love making me forget, but I was pretty sure it was Shasta siphoning off what was left of my sanity. I gave up and sat back in my seat with a sigh.

"Something wrong?" Super Agent asked, putting the movie on pause.

He was dressed casually, which meant that his dress shirt was unbuttoned at the collar and his sleeves were rolled up. We were at my place, sitting close together on the couch, but not as close as I wanted to be.

I was trying this new thing: self-control. It was all part of the realization I'd had when Super Agent and I had first met that I might have a teeny-tiny impulse-control issue. It had all started with me being framed for a murder I didn't commit and ended with me on probation. It turns out there's no law on the books for kicking your dead, cheating, Arizona state senator ex-boyfriend in the nuts, but there is one for disturbing a crime scene. If I hadn't caught Chuck Puckett's murderer for the FBI, I'd be sitting in jail right now facing an additional weapons charge instead of sitting on my couch on probation.

Super Agent and I had kinda, sorta already ripped each other's clothes off within days of meeting each other. Well, within days of *my* meeting *him*. He'd been following me for a year as part of a case the FBI had been putting together against Chuck Puckett. So while Super Agent knew everything, and I mean *everything*, about me, I was learning about him the old-fashioned way. One chaste date at a time.

My little impulse-control thing combined with a very slight anger-management issue meant that I had a lot of work to do. So this was me turning over a new leaf, becoming a better person, working on me, yada yada yada. And it wasn't humbling, noble or life affirming.

It was freaking frustrating as hell.

"I have a headache and can't find my pill case," I answered, releasing the tangled mass that was my hair from its ponytail and running my hands through it. Thanks to my Spanish/Armenian/Greek heritage I had thick, dark hair that hung down to my waist.

Super Agent loved my hair. Which was ironic seeing as how he didn't have any. He was bald, black, and so beautiful I couldn't look at him straight on without wanting to throw out all of my so-called self-improvement.

He watched my hair sift through my fingers like some men would watch a porn flick. "Want me to rub your head?"

"Oh, that would be heaven."

He put a pillow in his lap and patted it. "Lie down."

I did as he asked. He lifted my hair so that it draped out behind me. His fingers were magic. I groaned and he shifted me in his lap. After a few moments I noticed he hadn't turned the movie back on.

"Don't you want to see what happens?"

"I'm pretty sure they're going to have a fight because he did something stupid, then he'll make some big gesture to win her back. The end."

"Next time you can pick the movie."

"Deal. What's got you so stressed?"

I filled him in on my charming new employee. I got to the part about Shasta rubbing her ass on poor old lady Landers, and he burst out laughing.

"You're kidding."

"I wish I was."

The doorbell rang.

"You expecting someone?" Super Agent asked.

"Probably Miguel wanting to borrow something." I rolled off the couch and went to the door. "Like money or my car...again."

Nope. Not my brother.

A deliveryman held a huge vase of red roses. "Maggie Mae Castro?"

"Oh," I sighed. If my self-control was weak before, it now lay on its back with X's for eyes. Super Agent was gonna get so lucky.

Super Agent pressed against my back. "What's this?"

"Sign here." The delivery dude handed me a clipboard, which I scribbled on and passed back. He gave me the flowers, which weighed a ton. "Have a nice night."

"Thank you." I hefted the roses over to my dining room table and set them down. I leaned down and inhaled their scent. "Mmm." I *loved* roses. I looked up to see Super Agent on my porch, hands on hips.

He came back inside and slammed the door. "Who are those from?" His tone had an edge I didn't like.

"What the hell do you mean who are they from?"

"I'd like to know who's sending *my* girlfriend flowers." He actually thumped his chest on the word *my*.

I might have gone all gushy inside at his possessive use of the word *girlfriend* if it wasn't for the accusing look he was giving me.

"Must be from my *other boyfriend*. The one who sends me flowers."

He lunged for the card, but I snatched it away just in

time.

It was like watching a lion puff himself up for battle. He even roared. *"Who are they from?"*

"Obviously not from you!" And *why* weren't they from him? What the hell?

His nostrils flared, and if it was possible, he got even bigger. "Maggie," he warned.

I put a hand up and glared. When I was sure he wasn't going to grab for the card again, I opened it. Well, that was anticlimactic. I turned the card over, then pinched the envelope open, thinking I'd missed something.

He grabbed the card out of my hand and read it. His dark complexion reddened as he shook the card in my face. "I'm going to ask you one more time, who these are from?"

"I have no idea. I thought they were from you. Obviously I was wrong." I got mad all over again. "And why haven't you ever given me flowers?"

"What?" He shook his head. "That's not the point here."

I crossed my arms over my chest. "I think it's a darn good point."

"I'll buy you some freaking flowers already."

"Well, I don't want them *now*. They'd just be guilt flowers."

He slapped the notecard down on the table and pointed at the flowers, which had lost all their specialness since I'd thought they'd been from Super Agent. Now they kind of freaked me out.

"Who sent these?"

"I told you, *I don't know.*"

"I don't like this." His tone scattered goose bumps up my spine. It was his FBI-Special-Agent voice.

"What do you think it means?"

"I think it means someone likes you. A lot."

We silently glanced down at the crumpled, unsigned note on the table.

YOU'RE MINE, MAGGIE

I had a secret admirer with excellent taste, a pissed-off, paranoid boyfriend who carried a gun, a raging headache on stilettos named Shasta who was just now strolling in from an all-nighter, and *no aspirin* because my pill case was *still* missing. And no sex. Did I mention the no sex?

My life was awesome.

Shasta had managed to do nothing at all her first day, called in sick her second day, and now she was half an hour late for her third day. I'd begged Daryl to fire her, but he'd slinked away, mumbling something about disciplinary actions and giving chances and maybe a little something about the thickness of *my* personnel file.

"Why does she even bother to show up?" Tabitha whispered across the counter.

I just shook my head as I moved on to the next waiting customer. The other two E.L. beauty consultants and I were two deep at the counter and short a beauty consultant—Shasta. Estelle Landers only had a gift with purchase twice a year so we were swamped.

Shasta came over to me as I was ringing up my customer. "I'm like getting a latte? Soooo...." Her usual pixie voice was dotted with gravel—from her all-nighter, no doubt.

"Actually. No. You're not. You were supposed to be here at nine to help restock the counter. Soooo *like* guess what?" I grabbed her hand and slapped a list into it. "Go to the stockroom and bring back every piece of these products we have in stock."

"But I like *need* my latte?"

"No. What you need to do is breathe your smoker's breath in the stockroom while you get these products." I jutted out a hip and parked my hand on it, my best *I mean business* pose. "*Like* now."

"Whatever. You don't have to like go all bitch-faced at me?" She stomped off toward the stockroom.

"I'll show you bitch-faced, you little—"

"Careful," Tabitha warned, catching my raised fist. "I heard old man Stratford's in the store today. Our numbers came in and we're number one out all of his department stores. He's here to find out what we're doing different."

"Have you seen him yet?"

She shook her head. "He started on the first floor, but he'll be up here any minute. You punching out Shasta would not be the best first impression as a brand-new counter manager."

"Yeah, yeah, yeah." And it would kinda ruin all the self-improvement progress I've been trying so hard to make, not to mention jeopardize my probation. But it sure would feel good. I shoved my hand in my pocket to grab my favorite lipstick so I could do a quick reapply. It was gone. "Darn it." Not my lipstick too.

"What's wrong?"

"Nothing. I'll see you at—" I was cut off by a huge crashing sound that rocked the floor. "What the hell? Did that come from the stockroom?"

"I think so."

I rolled my eyes at Shasta's stupidity. "I am so going to kill that girl."

I ran around the counter with Tabitha on my heels.

Our stockroom was in the handbag department and all of their sales staff had come over to see what had happened. I punched in the code to the door and turned the handle. The door wouldn't budge.

"Shasta?" I called out. No answer. I turned to the crowd standing around. "Help me push the door. Something's fallen in front of it."

We shoved and shoved until we created a space big enough that I could poke my head through. "Oh, my God. Shasta!" I pulled my head out. "Push harder. Somebody call 9-1-1!"

We gave it everything we had and finally made enough headway that I could shove my fat behind through. Tabitha slipped easily into the stockroom behind me. It was worse up close than it had been from the doorway. Somebody behind me screamed.

One of the fifteen-foot-high metal shelving units had fallen over. I could just barely see the top of Shasta's head. The big boxes on the higher shelves had piled down onto her and in front of the door. I started pulling boxes off of her, handing them back to the people behind me.

I finally moved the last big box. "Oh, dang."

Behind me the gawkers gasped. Someone was crying. The shelving unit had pinned Shasta to the wall, hitting her square in the solar plexus. Her head hung on her chest, a thin line of blood seeped from her mouth.

"Shasta?"

Licking my lips, I reached out a tentative hand and felt for a pulse. Nothing. I'd seen death before when Chuck Puckett had been murdered. It really hadn't prepared me for this. Bowing my head, I closed my eyes. I whispered a quick blessing and made the sign of the cross. I wasn't the best person or the best Catholic, but it was all I could think to do for her.

"What's the trouble here?" a male voice I didn't recognize asked.

I stood up slowly and turned to the crowd that had gathered in the cramped space, thinking I should probably get everyone out of there.

An older gentleman, whose portrait hung in the executive offices of every Stratford's Department Store, broke from the crowd and rushed forward. "Shasta?"

Oh, hell no.

He elbowed me aside and dropped to his knees. "Shasta!" He shook her. "Shasta!"

"I'm sorry—" I began.

"Don't just stand there. Get this thing off her!" He tried to move the shelving unit, but it wouldn't budge.

I put a hand on his arm. "Mr. Stratford, don't. There's no way to move it. Help is already on the way."

"You don't understand." He leaned against the unit, putting his whole body into it. It didn't shift an inch. He bent over and gripped his knees, breathing hard. "I can't leave her like this." He looked up at me and whispered, "She's...she's my daughter."

Dread pooled, sick and thick in my belly. Oh, dang. Double dang. Shoot, frick, dang!

I'd killed the big boss's daughter.

*T*his was going to look really bad in my personnel file. My first month as counter manager and I'd gotten one of my employees killed. And not just any employee, but the storeowner's daughter. I should've let her go get her latte like she wanted. If I had, she'd be happily texting and sipping, I'd be unhappily brooding and working my ass off, the store would be open, cops wouldn't be swarming the place, and no one would be carting a body bag out the door. But nooo, I had to go and assert my stupid authority.

At least I knew now how Shasta had gotten a job she wasn't qualified for or interested in and why Daryl hadn't fired her.

Xavier put his arm across my shoulders. "Well, at least old man Stratford knows who you are now."

I gave him a get-bent glare. I hadn't shared Mr. Stratford's little revelation with Tabitha and Xavier. Not long after the police had arrived, Mr. Stratford had pulled me aside and insisted—no, insisted was too nice a word, *threatened* was really more accurate—me not to tell anyone Shasta was his daughter.

"It's really not your fault," Tabitha offered.

I transferred the glare to her. "You're almost convincing."

"That's not what I meant. I mean it's totally not your fault. How were you supposed to know that shelving unit was going to fall on her? Who could know that? No one. That's who. I wouldn't have known. You couldn't have known."

I put a hand up to stop her. Tabitha always jibber-jabbered when she was nervous.

"I bet her family could sue for the shelves not being strapped to the wall," Xavier said.

I swiveled my head in his direction. "What?"

"No strapping. Didn't you notice?"

Come to think of it, I had, but I guessed I'd been so distracted by Daddy Department Store's declaration and threatening aside that the shelves not being bolted to the wall had kinda taken a backseat. Why hadn't that shelving unit been fixed to the wall?

Lance strolled over and inserted himself between Tabitha and me. "Terrible tragedy. Terrible." He slipped an arm around my waist and pulled me to him. "How're you holding up, love?"

Xavier tightened his hold and brought me closer to him. He hated Lance. "She's fine."

"Indeed she is." Lance dug his fingers into the flesh on my hip and jerked me closer. "Now that I'm here."

I suddenly found myself the center of a tug of war, my head bobbing back and forth. I finally had enough of them and elbowed them in the sides. "If one of you tries to pee on me, you'll both be pissing sideways for the rest of your lives. Knock it off."

They dropped their arms.

Xavier crossed his over his chest. "She was fine *before* you got here," he grumbled at Lance.

My retort caught in my throat as they brought Shasta's body out of the stockroom and hefted the body bag onto a stretcher. Even though she was nearly as tall as me at five foot nine, the black bag seemed too big for her young body.

The nervous chitchat was suspended for a moment as we all watched them wheel her body out of the store.

"Why was she even over on that side of the stockroom?" Lance's voice held the same disbelief we were all feeling.

For once His Fake Highness was making sense. Annoying, tactless sense, but sense nonetheless. The shelving unit that had fallen on Shasta held Shy Kitty products, not Estelle Landers. Our products were on the other side of the stockroom. So what had made her turn right instead of left?

"Maybe she saw something shiny and climbed up for a closer look." Tabitha clapped a hand over her mouth, her eyes wide. "I can't believe I just disrespected the dead like that."

"Did you or one of your counter mates ask Shasta to get some product down for you?" I asked Xavier.

"No. We pulled stock this morning."

Curiouser and curiouser. The shelves weren't attached to the wall like they were supposed to be. Shasta had been on the wrong side of the stockroom at the wrong time. There was a seldom-used door at the other end of the stockroom. Someone could've lured her in, brought the shelving unit down on top of her and then easily escaped. Everything about this "accident" just didn't feel right to me, like the very real possibility that it hadn't been an accident at all. That maybe, just maybe someone had unstrapped that shelving unit and used it to kill.

I caught Mr. Stratford staring at me across the sales floor, the look in his eyes wary and watchful as I worked to close down the counter for the day. Did he suspect as I did that his daughter had been murdered? And if so, why keep the fact that Shasta was his daughter a secret? Wouldn't that help the police find out who killed her and why? Maybe she was killed in retaliation for something Mr. Stratford had or hadn't done. Maybe her murder was some kind of warning to him. Or maybe—and this was kinda farfetched—he killed Shasta, setting it up to *look* like an accident.

Or the more likely scenario was that having a murdered ex-boyfriend made me see conspiracies where there was nothing more than lazy workmanship and a father distancing himself from his drugged-up screw-up of a daughter. But that wasn't nearly as interesting to me, so I was going with "Murder for a Thousand, Alex".

"The police want to interview you," Daryl said, drawing me out of my conspiracy theories. He was in red because it was Wednesday. "There's a detective waiting in my office to speak with you."

Yeah, I didn't do cops. Unless you counted Super Agent. Him I'd do upside down and sideways on a trapeze in the rain. "Can't I just write down what I saw and give it to him?

You know, like a report?" I hated reports, but I hated cops more. They gave me hives. I'd already starting itching like an addict coming down off a fix.

He reached up and squeezed my elbow, real concern on his face. I didn't know he could do concern or any other kind of emotion other than avoidance. "I'm sorry you have to go through this. I wish there was a way I could take your place. Do you want me to go in there with you...as support?"

I blinked down at him. This was the nicest he'd ever been to me. "Thanks. That's really sweet of you, but I can handle this." I glanced up at his closed office door. "I guess."

He bowed his head, cleared his throat and gave my elbow another squeeze before letting go. "I'm always here for you," he mumbled.

Shuffling my feet, I glanced anywhere but at him. "Yeah, sure. Okay." Tragedy did strange things to people I guessed, like turning them into human beings.

As I headed off toward Daryl's office, I could feel Mr. Stratford's eyes still on me. The look on his face was almost pleading. Did he really think I'd spill my guts under pressure like some cheap 99-cent store piñata? Well, he'd see I was made of sterner stuff. And why I cared what that man thought of me was beyond me. Other than wanting to keep my job in his store I had no reason to be afraid of him. So why was I sweating through my clinical-strength antiperspirant?

I knocked on Daryl's office door, then pushed it open without waiting for a reply. "You wanted to speak with me?"

Oh, cripes. Not another hot one. Really, whoever was doing the law-enforcement recruiting these days was better than a casting agent for a nighttime TV drama. This one was long and lean with the lazy-eyed squint of a young Elvis. His dark hair and goatee shined blue-black under the fluorescent lights. Suddenly I was sweating for a whole other reason.

"Maggie Mae Castro?" Da-yam that voice.

"That's me. How long is this going to take?" I made a show of checking the time on my cell phone. "I've got plans." I said this to remind myself. Plans = date. Date = boyfriend. Boyfriend = can't throw myself at him like the sex-starved slut I was.

"Have a seat." He smiled, but there was something not quite right about it and the look in his eyes that accompanied it. "I'll try not to keep you. I'm Detective Cruz. I just have few questions about what happened today."

He asked me for my contact info, then took me through what had happened with Shasta. It was all very conversational and inappropriately flirty. My hives hardly itched at all until he asked me who had access to the stockroom.

"Anyone in the cosmetics department. They haven't changed the access code since I started here three years ago. Why?"

"In the past few days, did you see anyone hanging around the stockroom who shouldn't have been?"

Honestly, I hardly paid attention to anything other than keeping my sales numbers up and how long until I was off work. "No."

"Can you think of anything that seemed unusual or out of place to you?"

"No." I didn't think he'd care about all the crap I'd misplaced over the past few weeks.

"Okay, well, thank you for answering my questions. If you can think of anything else—" he handed me his business card, "—give me a call."

"This wasn't an accident, was it?"

He sat back in his seat and regarded me with his sexy, panty-melting bedroom eyes. "Why do you ask?"

I shrugged. "Why are you answering my question with a question?"

"Why won't you tell me why you think this wasn't an

accident?"

"Why don't I call you if I have any more questions?" I got up from my chair and headed for the door.

"Are you seeing anyone?"

Halting midstride, I turned back to look at him. My initial attraction to him had slowly morphed into unease the more time I'd spent with him. Even if I wasn't deliciously tangled up with Super Agent there was no way I'd go out with this guy. "I'm not seeing enough of someone."

He laughed, but it had an odd edge to it. "What does that mean?"

"It means I'm not in the market for any more frustration. But thank you." I opened the door and paused. "Oh, and thanks for answering my question."

"What question?"

"The one about this not being an accident."

"I never said that."

"Actually, you did. I've gotten pretty fluent in verbal evasion." And I had a big ole broad-shouldered FBI agent to thank for that. "Nice meeting you."

Heading back to the counter to gather my things and go home, I thought about all Detective Cruz had said and not said. Shasta's death wasn't accidental, so who wanted her dead?

*I*nstead of grabbing my purse and heading home like I should've done, I went in search of Mr. Stratford. He wasn't where I last saw him so I took the elevator to the third floor. The executive offices were tucked behind an unmarked door next to giftwrap. I figured if Daddy Department Store was still in the store that was where I'd find him.

Callie, the store manager's assistant, was busy fielding calls at her desk. I had to wait a couple of minutes for a break in calls. The media had already gotten wind of the story, apparently. "Hey, Callie, is Mr. Stratford up here?"

She flicked a hand toward one of the offices that had become vacant during the last store restructuring. "In there. But he asked to not be disturbed." She let out a hefty sigh as her phone lit up again.

I waited until she answered to tiptoe past her. "I won't disturb him." Much.

I did my usual knock-and-burst-in thing, opening the door to find Mr. Stratford hunched over the desk, head in hands.

He lifted his head. "I told you... What do *you* want?"

Yeah, I wasn't happy to see him either.

"Can we talk?" I closed the door behind me.

"No."

"Then I'll talk. You can do whatever." I lowered myself into the chair across the desk from him. It was then that I noticed his red-rimmed eyes and mussed-up hair. In all the confusion and shock I'd forgotten this man had lost his daughter. "I'm sorry about Shasta."

"If that's why you barged in here, you're wasting your time as well as mine."

"It's not, but that doesn't mean I don't mean it." Putting my elbows on my knees, I leaned closer. "I'm sorry."

He glanced down at his hands on the desk. "You're the first person to offer condolences."

"If more people knew about Shasta's connection to you—"

"No."

"Okaaay." I didn't get this guy. He obviously cared about his daughter, so why not claim her?

"Do you have children?"

"Not that I know of."

That managed to pull a half smile out of him. "I didn't think I did either until about fifteen years ago."

By my quick calculations—math genius that I was—Shasta was about three when Stratford had found out he was a baby daddy. Sooo Shasta clearly hadn't been a product of his twenty-eight-year marriage. No wonder he wasn't so keen on making the news public.

He noted my raised brows. "I'm not proud of myself. I did the best I could, providing for her, making sure she had everything she needed."

"Your wife doesn't know."

"I didn't want to hurt her. We couldn't have children. If she found out about Shasta... Look, I love my wife."

I held up a hand. He didn't owe me an explanation. "I get it."

"I did the best I could for Shasta. She got into drugs. I paid for rehab. She got arrested. I got her a job."

"Yeah, thanks for that."

He had the good sense to look embarrassed. "Sorry. She chose cosmetics. I thought maybe if she worked at something she enjoyed—" He let out a frustrated breath. "I kept tabs. I know how that went. I'm sorry you had to deal with her...behavior."

"The police don't think it was an accident."

That seemed to surprise him. "What else could it be?" The realization slowly dawned for him. "No," he breathed. "Why? Who would want to hurt her like that? She was just a troubled girl."

"It happened in your store..." Really, this man was a department store mogul, but he couldn't put two and two together?

"You think...aw, Jesus." He scrubbed his hands over his face.

"Who knew Shasta was your daughter?"

"No one. Well, her mother, obviously. My attorneys...and now you. My name isn't even on her birth certificate. We did everything privately and quietly. Her mother just wanted to secure Shasta's financial future."

"Could Shasta have told someone?"

"She didn't know about me. It was a condition of my contract with her mother, Valerie. I always deal with Valerie directly. All Shasta knew was that she got the job here at the store through one of Valerie's friends. We've never even met."

Wow. No wonder Shasta had been so screwed up.

"Is there anyone who might have a grudge against you or the store?"

He shook his head. "No. I can't think of anyone who could or would do such a thing. God. I still can't believe this. I guess I should call Valerie and break the news."

There was a knock at the door.

"Yes?" Mr. Stratford answered.

Callie opened the door and popped her head around it. "There's a detective here to speak with you, Mr. Stratford."

"I'll be there in a moment." He waited until Callie had closed the door. "Please. Don't tell anyone what I've told you. My wife...her health is very fragile."

I'd heard about Mrs. Stratford's cancer battle. "I won't, but don't you think the police should know? You know, to help them find Shasta's killer?"

He flinched at the word *killer*, then battled back, morphing into the titan of department store industry. "That's my decision to make. Not yours. I need your word you won't talk about this with anyone."

I rolled my eyes at him. So dramatic. "I gave you my word."

"I suppose you think you've got me over a barrel now, that I'll do anything to keep you from telling my secret."

"I'm not going to blackmail you, if that's what you're implying. Like you said, it's your story to tell or not tell."

"Why don't I believe you?"

"You're a cynical old bastard?"

His laugh surprised me. "I object to being called *old*."

I rose and headed for the door. With my hand on the knob, I turned back and gave him a wink. "Sorry to be the one to break it to you."

"Thank you."

Now I was the one caught off guard. "For what?"

He made a sweeping gesture.

"You're welcome," I answered. "Let me know what the arrangements for Shasta will be. I'd like to be there."

"You don't have to."

"I know." I opened the door and nearly walked smack dab into Detective Cruz, catching myself with a hand on his hot, hard chest. I quickly snatched it away. "Er, sorry." I stepped to the side and back out onto the sales floor, but the detective caught up to me at the elevator.

"I guess I know now why I got shot down."

Was he... Did he...? Oh, *hell* no. I folded my arms across my chest to keep myself from smacking that smug smile off his face and stared hard at the numbers above the elevator door.

"You recently got a promotion, didn't you?" He moved in front of me. "From what I've learned the big boss man set Shasta Devereaux up with a job here. Maybe you didn't like being replaced with a younger, hotter version of yourself." He shook his head and *tsk*ed. "Messy business pitting your mistresses against each other. Maybe he was hoping for a catfight. Some men like that kind of thing."

"You're an ass."

"So maybe you decided to take out the competition."

I stared at him, balling my hands into fists, my face growing hot.

He inclined his head toward the office. "Was that you securing your position?" He made a rude hand gesture, moving his fisted hand back and forth from his mouth while poking his tongue against the inside of his cheek. "Assuming the position under his desk?"

Before I'd even formed the thought to do it, I cracked him across the cheek with the flat of my hand. His head jerked back. The sound of my palm slapping his face reverberated around us. Suddenly I found myself plastered against the metal elevator door, my arm twisted painfully behind my back. He caught my other wrist and brought it back to join my other one. His long, hard body pressed against my back, trapping me. I couldn't breathe.

His hot breath blew across the side of my face. "That's assaulting an officer." He kicked my feet wide apart. "But then maybe you like it rough."

He held both of my hands in one of his. Even if I wanted to I couldn't twist away. He was too heavy and too strong. I sucked in a breath as he ran his other hand over my body, slowing at the parts he seemed to especially like. The click of handcuffs jumpstarted my heart into a hard rhythm. He did the whole frisking thing again, this time with both hands. His hands started to slide up my skirt.

Twisting, I elbowed him in the ear. "Go ahead and try it." I sounded braver than I felt. "There are cameras all over this store. I won't need a job at all when I sue you and the Scottsdale PD for sexual assault."

He jerked me hard by the arm as the elevator doors opened, his handsome face twisted with lines of cruelty. "Maggie Mae Castro, you're under arrest."

Yeah, this wasn't the first time I'd heard those words and it likely wouldn't be the last.

7

I sat in a jail cell next to a woman who could crack nearly every joint in her body. She'd started at her neck and worked her way down, then up again. It was rather fascinating how she shifted her pelvis to pop her hip joints, but the noise her knees made was kinda sickening. She was just beginning her show again from the top when Super Agent appeared.

"Really? Assaulting an officer? That's a new one for you."

I eased into a standing position and sidled up to the bars, careful not to move too quickly. Man, was I glad to see him. "I only wish I'd gone for his nuts." I swept out a hand, indicating my lovely cell. "It would've made my time here so much more worthwhile."

A guard came over and opened the cell door. "You're free to go."

I slipped through the opening and slammed into Super Agent, hugging him hard. "Thank you for springing me."

He held me back just as hard. I sucked in a breath and shifted so that his arms hit a different spot.

"You're welcome," he said. "I owe Detective Cruz for dropping the charges and not notifying your probation officer."

I pushed out of his arms. "No." Rattling the cell door, I

called for the guard to come back. "I'd rather rot in this cell than owe that sadistic bastard anything."

Super Agent's attention snapped to my wrist. He jerked at my sleeve, revealing dark red welts and cuts where the cuffs had bit in. He pulled my hands free from the bars and examined them. "What the hell?"

I just stared stubbornly at him, my cheeks hot, my eyes stinging.

Detective Cruz had enjoyed hurting me.

Super Agent's voice got very scary. "Where else?"

Pressing my lips together, I fixed my gaze on his and shook my head. He gently took my elbow and towed me to the end of the hall, out a door and into a bathroom. As soon as he closed and locked the door, he reached behind me and slid down the zipper at the back of my dress. I let him. Easing it off my shoulders and down my arms, he got his first look at what Cruz's "favor" had cost.

"Son of a bitch."

I didn't dare look. If it looked as bad as it felt, I wouldn't be able to keep it together. The last thing I wanted was to show any weakness here at the police station where I might run into Cruz and he'd see it. He never saw me cry. No matter what he did, I hadn't given him the satisfaction.

"Did he...?"

I shook my head so Super Agent didn't have to say it. No, Cruz hadn't raped me. I didn't know why he hadn't. He could've. I'd been handcuffed and helpless, and he'd been extremely pissed off.

Super Agent brought me carefully into his chest, with a hand at the back of my head and the other around my waist. I flinched when his finger hit the bump on the base of my skull. Pulling back to watch my face, he gingerly ran his fingers over my scalp, his full lips pressed flat.

"That's the only one," I told him. "I think."

He nodded and helped me put my dress back on. I couldn't read his expression. Other than the occasional jaw tick and grim set to his mouth, he gave nothing away. When I was finally put back together, he took my hand and kissed the back of it, then led me out of the bathroom without another word.

The next couple of hours went by in a blur. After Super Agent spoke to Cruz's commanding officer, he took me to the hospital where I was examined. Photos were taken. Questions were asked. I couldn't look at Super Agent during that part.

He never said anything and never left my side. I thought I'd been holding it together for me because I'm just that stubborn, but really I'd kept a tight rein on my emotions for Super Agent. It was almost like a competition. When I felt him coming close to losing it, I put more steel in my spine and resolve in my tone. When my voice wobbled, he visibly tensed, giving me the strength I needed to power through.

When I was released, Super Agent drove me home. We hadn't spoken more than the necessary words to each other since he'd come to bail me out of jail. We got to my house and found a plain brown box about the size of a shoebox on my doormat. Probably those shoes I shouldn't have ordered but were too cute to resist. Super Agent picked it up and set it on the coffee table for me when we went inside.

"Thanks for...everything." I tried for cheery, clasping my hands together and pasting on a smile. "I was thinking of ordering a pizza if you want to stay. Or if you have plans, that's cool."

"I'll stay."

"Okay, well." This was awkward. "If you want to go ahead and order the pizza, I'm fine with whatever." I hooked a thumb down the hall behind me. "I'm just going to take a shower and wash off the prison funk." I started to back up. "There's wine on the counter and beer in the fridge. Just help yourself."

"Do you need any help?"

"No. I'm good. Been taking a shower on my own for a while now."

"Maggie?"

I'd turned to go down the hall, but his voice brought me back around. "Yeah?"

He looked around the room as if it might give him a clue as to what he wanted to say. Finally his gaze landed back on me. "Could I stay with you while you take a shower?"

I tilted my head to the side.

He rubbed a hand over his smooth head. "I'm not asking to...you know. I'll just lean against the counter or sit on the toilet lid and keep you company. If you want."

Now it was my turn to search for words, but I couldn't come up with any so I just nodded and headed down the hall. He followed. I turned the water on and started to undress. He stood just outside the bathroom door, his face averted. He'd seen me in my underwear. Heck, he'd seen me fully naked on one occasion and been nose to skin with my body. His chivalry was sweet.

As soon as I'd climbed in and closed the shower curtain, I heard Super Agent lower the toilet lid and sit down. Tipping my head back and closing my eyes, I let the hot water flow over me. And that was when everything hit me. I buckled under the weight of the images that crashed over me. *His* face, the way he'd smelled, the ugly things he'd said...and done. The pain. Gasping, I swiped a blind hand out for purchase, hitting the shower curtain. Super Agent caught it, then stepped in and caught me.

Wrapping myself around him, I gripped handfuls of his shirt, needing his solidity. The water beat down on us, soaking his clothes. He held me, whispering nonsense to me as I tried to catch my breath. I fought hard. I wasn't going to break down. I wasn't going to let that jerk get any more of me than he already had.

Somewhere along the way my lips found Super Agent's

and I kissed him as though I needed the feel of him to keep breathing. He kissed me back the same way. I don't know what happened to his clothes. It all got so frenzied and overwhelming. Hands were everywhere, his and mine. And then he lifted me, shut the water off, toweled us both off and carried me into the bedroom.

Ever so gently, he laid me on the bed. The look in his eyes made me flush, heating up my already oversensitized skin. He was so beautiful in the meager lamplight that for a moment I almost didn't think he was real. His gaze traveled over my body, taking in the bruises and marks between my tattoos.

"Don't," I warned. "Don't look at them."

"I'm not sure how to touch you."

I reached over and turned out the light, settling the darkness around us. "Now come here, close your eyes, and figure it the hell out."

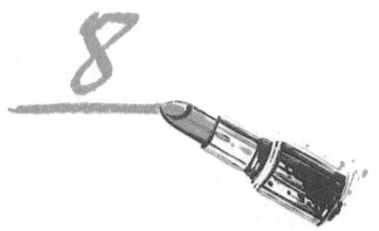

8

I've never been good at asking for favors even though I was often too generous when it came to granting them. I've never borrowed money other than from a bank. I've never gotten a pet or house plant so that I didn't have to ask anyone to take care of it when I went out of town. I've never asked anyone for help with anything. Ever.

But the night before I'd come so close to begging Super Agent to help me forget. Fortunately I didn't have to. Somehow he knew what I'd needed without me having to ask. His touch was a balm that soothed more than my fear—it smoothed out some of the roughest places inside me. He made me feel treasured. This man gave me what I couldn't and wouldn't ask for.

In the cold, pale light of morning, lying next to him, I wanted to reach out to him. It seemed that I wasn't done needing him and that scared the ever-living heck out of me.

Or maybe it was because this was an old pattern for me, getting swept away in the moment without thinking things through. I wanted to be with Super Agent. I did. But I didn't exactly have the best record where men were concerned. No looking before leaping for me. No, I was a dive headfirst kind of gal only to find out later there was no water, or if there was, it was infested with sharks.

I was supposed to be changing my life and my habits, and yet last night I'd slipped right back into them without a thought or backward glance. Part of me didn't regret it. But that part was an avid slut who'd loved every single minute of tangling the sheets with Super Agent. The other part of me, my practical side, was holding the umbrella of regret over the whole business, casting shadows over my enjoyment. She was an evil bitch who took the fun out of everything. She was also the one I should've listened to in the first place.

Sliding to the other side of the bed, careful not to wake Super Agent and face the morning-after good mornings, I climbed out and put on my robe, then went in search of coffee. My body complained, reminding me of what I'd been through yesterday. I still hadn't been able to bring myself to see the damage. Cleopatra had nothing on me.

While the coffee dripped I went to my small corner desk and opened my laptop. My email had exploded overnight. There were about twelve from Xavier. I groaned at one subject line: *Maggie's perp walk take #36*. Great. The reporters hovering outside the store must've caught Cruz dragging me out to his car.

I opened the email and clicked on the link. Yup. There I was in all my handcuffed glory. The video was choppy and grainy, but I could clearly make out the shouts of the reporters. It hadn't been that long since my last videoed perp walk when I was wrongly arrested for murdering Chuck Puckett. It seemed that the reporters hadn't forgotten me or the clever nickname they'd given me— *Murdering Maggie*.

Oh, yay. Someone had created a YourVid channel just for my perp walks. Some of them were duplicates, but still! There were nine videos in all. I groaned and deleted the rest of Xav's emails unopened. He was such a jerk.

Wait. I didn't remember sending myself an email. I opened it. What the...?

I stood up so fast I knocked the chair over. No. No, no, no, no, no. That couldn't be right.

"What's wrong?"

I turned to find a very naked Super Agent holding a big gun. And no, that wasn't a euphemism. Stunned beyond the ability to form words, I jabbed a finger at my computer.

He strode over and had a look for himself. "My dearest Maggie Mae," Super Agent read aloud, a deep frown settling between his dark eyes. "I've watched and worried about you. You've been so upset. I would do anything for you and so I have. Imitation is *not* the sincerest form of flattery. She had to go so I could see you smile once again. Remember...you're mine, Maggie. Only mine."

Super Agent's furious gaze met mine.

"Is he saying what I think he's saying?" I'd read it and had it read to me and I *still* couldn't believe it. *Why?* Why would someone do such a thing?

"That he killed your coworker because he's obsessed with you...yes."

Poor Shasta. Poor Mr. Stratford. Some maniac had killed Shasta because of me. Me. I was hardly worth obsessing over, let alone killing for. What had I done to attract and encourage this person? This was all my fault.

He pointed to the return email address. "How is this right? You sent the email to yourself?"

"No. Of course not. He must've hacked my account or sent it from my cell phone. My cell phone!" I rushed to my purse and started pawing through it. "Nooooo. Not my cell phone too."

"When was the last time you saw it? Wait. What do you mean not your cell phone too?"

"I've been misplacing things. Just little things...until now. Darn it."

"What kinds of little things?" He was using his FBI-Special-Agent voice again, questioning me like I was a witness before I'd even had my coffee. Not smart.

"Remember when I couldn't find my pill case? That's one thing. Ah, the lipstick I keep in my uniform pocket. The lucky Euro my ex-boyfriend Niccolo gave me when he took me to Italy. The hairband I always keep in my purse to put my hair up. A pair of earrings Chuck Puckett had given me that were also in my purse—"

"So things that you carried in your purse or on your person, correct?"

"Yeah, pretty much."

"Hmm."

"Hmm, what?"

"What does this part mean?" Super Agent pointed to the postscript at the bottom of the email. "What 'gift' is he talking about?"

At first I had no idea what he could be referring to, and then it hit me. I swiveled my head toward the package Super Agent had brought in that had been sitting on my porch last night. There it sat on my coffee table in all its creepy glory. Super Agent followed my gaze, then stomped over—still gloriously, fantastically naked, my slut side pointed out—and picked up the box with his non-gun-toting hand.

I averted my eyes and swished a hand at him. "Would you put that thing away?"

"I don't remembering you having an issue with guns."

"Yeah, no. You should probably put your gun away too."

He grunted a laugh and put the box back down. "Don't touch that."

While he went to cover himself up, I couldn't stop myself from tiptoeing over to the coffee table for a closer look at the package. I didn't recognize the neat block lettering. And unfortunately there was no return address like *Stalker McObssesion, 1234 Crazy Drive, Insane Town, AZ (come and get me!)*. That would've been a tremendous help.

Super Agent came back with a towel wrapped around

his waist and his wet clothes. "Can I put these in the dryer?"

Oh, right. I'd forgotten how he'd left his clothes in the tub when we'd erm...ah...you know. I took them from him and put them in to dry. When I got back he was sitting on the couch with the box open in front of him.

"Hey," I said. "You'd think I'd get to open my own present. It's not like I get very many."

He scowled at me as I sat down next to him. "You mean like trips to Italy and jewelry?" Well, when he put it like that, I guessed I did get the occasional bauble or two. "I'll buy you a present. Or three," he grumbled. He was so touchy on this subject. "*And* flowers."

"Well, gee, you sure know how to make a girl feel all gooshy and special."

"You think I like some sicko sending my girlfriend flowers and gifts?" He gestured toward the beautifully expensive box of chocolates nestled in gold tissue paper. "He's making me look bad," he complained.

That was the second time he'd called me that this week. We hadn't discussed the particulars of our relationship, preferring to zigzag back and forth in the nebulous *Going Out but Not Formally Committed Even Though We've Slept Together* zone.

"So...I'm your girlfriend?"

He picked up a ropey strand of my hair and twisted it around his finger, bringing me closer. "You got a problem with that?"

I shrugged.

"Most women would've nailed that down weeks ago."

"I'm not most women."

"No kidding. Anyone ever tell you that you have intimacy issues?"

"Oh, do tell me about them, Mr. No-Talk-Unless-I-Absolutely-Have-To."

"I'm a guy. We don't do chat."

I looked down to where his towel gaped, displaying how very much a guy he was. I pointed at his crotch. "You got a permit for that?"

He readjusted the towel. "What was I saying about intimacy issues?"

"I showed you intimate last night."

"No. You showed me avoidance." He released my hair and clasped my hand. "When are you going to talk about what happened yesterday?"

"I talked about it."

"Not with me."

"Can I eat the chocolates?"

"No." He squeezed my hand. "Avoidance."

I rolled my eyes and huffed out a breath.

"We're going to have to report the email, missing items, and the presents to the police. They might be able to track down your phone if he still has it."

"Do I have to be here?" I wasn't super excited to be in a room with cops again even though I'd essentially had one in my bed last night.

"Yes, but I'll be with you."

I nodded. "All right. If you're there. But you can't leave."

"Why don't you go get dressed? I'll take care of everything here."

I got up and headed for the hall, then turned back. "Hey, ah...about last night. You gave me something better than any present. And I'm not talking about the—" I made a back-and-forth gesture between us, blushing like a virgin, "—you know. So...thanks. For that. And the other thing. The other thing was good too." Clearly I didn't excel at gratitude either. "You don't have to buy me a gift. Not that I wouldn't love getting presents from you just...you know...don't kill anyone for me."

*T*he good news was that I found my cell phone and the FBI was getting involved. This was now a computer-hacking incident, as someone had hacked into my computer to send the email through my own account. The FBI being all up in my business—*again*—also might have had a little something to do with Super Agent being pissed off that a murdering bastard was hassling his girlfriend. *And* giving her presents. Would he ever let that go?

The bad news was that I found my cell phone and the FBI was getting involved. My voicemail was jam-packed with messages from reporters, salivating over the news of my arrest, the charges I'd brought against Cruz, *and* the FBI's involvement in Shasta's murder. Evil ninjas! Everyone wanted a piece of me, including the FBI, which had taken my computer, my statement, and way too much of my free time. More paperwork had been added to my brick-thick FBI file. Yay.

Daryl called to let me know that Stratford's department store was still closed because of the ongoing investigation but would probably reopen tomorrow. So no work for me. Xavier wouldn't stop texting me, much to Super Agent's annoyance. My mother had gotten wind of my arrest and so I had to endure an endless lecture about responsibility and all the disgrace I'd brought down on the family. Of course no mention was made of my brother and *his* multiple brushes with the law. On top of all of that, Super Agent had taken it upon himself to hover over me like a nervous, new mother. Again.

This feeling of déjà vu was starting to feel all too familiar.

"Your place or mine?" Super Agent asked as we climbed into his car outside the Phoenix FBI office.

I was twitchy and on edge, having spent way more time with law-enforcement types than I could handle in the past couple of days. Even Super Agent was starting to scrape against my shredded nerves.

"I really just want to go home," I answered.

"Okay, we'll stop at my place and I'll pack a bag."

"Are you going somewhere?" Seemed kind of inconvenient given what was happening, but okaaayyyyy.

"I'm staying with you."

"Whoa." I put my hands up palms out. "Slow this ride down. Since when did knocking together and calling me your girlfriend mean moving in together?"

He ticked off points on his hand. "This guy knows where you live. He's stolen from you. He's hacked into your email account. Who knows what else he knows about you and how he's going to use it. He's so obsessed with you he killed somebody for you."

My slut side got distracted by his big hands, remembering how skilled they were. She wanted to know why I was turning down the chance to have those hands on me again. I was beginning to come around to her way of thinking. Almost. Maybe. Her argument was flawless.

My practical side threw a flag on the play. *Hello! Murderer after you! Protection!*

"I get all that," I said, hating my practical side. "But I don't think you staying at my place is such a good idea."

He studied me for a moment. "It's about last night, isn't

it?"

"No." His FBI-Special-Agent gaze practically drilled a hole in me. "Sort of." I really didn't want to talk about this. "Yes," I finally blurted out. "Okay?"

"You regret what happened."

"Regret wouldn't be the word I'd use." But it was close.

"What would the word be?"

I thought on it for a moment. "Rethinking."

"Rethinking." Now it was his turn to be contemplative. After a couple of moments he nodded. "Okay. Can I ask why?"

I pulled my sleeve up and pointed to the tattoo I had of a bunch of forget-me-nots with ribbon-wrapped stems on my forearm. "Read this."

"The flowers?"

"Look at the words in the shading of the ribbon."

"'I will make better mistakes tomorrow,'" he read. When he looked up at me I couldn't quite pin down the expression he wore. "Is that what you think it was, a mistake?"

How to explain? "The same part of my brain that thought last night was a good idea—" I moved my finger to the handcuff marks on my wrists, "—also thought it was a good idea to question a pissed-off cop's ability to get it up while I was handcuffed in his backseat."

He leaned back in his seat, disbelief parting his lips. "You're comparing being with me last night to what that asshole cop did to you?"

"No." Oh crap, this wasn't going well. "This isn't going well."

He just stared at me. Uh-oh. I'd hurt his feelings. And pissed him off. The anger was just now fading in across his features.

"I got the tattoo hoping it would remind me not to act on impulse," I tried to explain. I really sucked at this touchy-feely stuff.

He continued to watch me. At least he hadn't kicked me out of his car. Yet.

"I've been told I might have anger-management issues. And a slight impulse-control issue. I'm trying to improve myself." I paused for applause. Yeah, no. He clearly wasn't impressed.

His gaze unnerved me, which was probably the point. I didn't want to hurt him or make him think I regretted being with him. What I regretted was not taking a moment to make the conscious choice to be with him. Flying high on emotion, I'd just wanted to trade one memory for another much better one.

"I just wanted different hands on me," I told him in a rush, shame heating my cheeks. "Can you understand that?"

"Yeah," he said after a moment, sagging a little in his seat. "I can."

It was my turn to stare at him. I wish I knew what he was thinking. I also wished I could thank him for muddling through my lame-assed explanation and for making the effort to understand it. Especially since I could hardly make sense of it myself.

"I'm trying not to feel used," he said. "I get it. I really do. I just wish it had meant the same to us both."

Oh. *Ouch.* "I thought I was the girl in this relationship." I clapped my hand over my mouth, then mumbled under it. "I'm so sorry. I didn't mean that." Stupid impulse issues! "It did mean something to me. I swear. Honestly, I don't even know why you stick around sometimes."

"You have your charms." He reached out and did that thing where he wrapped my hair around his finger. "How about next time we plan ahead so we're both on the same page at the same time?"

I lowered my hand and gave him the side-eye. "You want to make an appointment with me for sex?"

"Not exactly. I want you to tell me when you're ready. Ahead of time. No impulsive decisions. No regrets or rethinking." He made a back-and-forth motion between us. "Same page."

"Okay. But doesn't that take some of the fun out of it?"

He leaned in, a wicked smile curving his mouth. "No. It gives me time to think up new ways to make you scream."

"I don't think you should move in with me," I told Super Agent on the drive back to Scottsdale.

I had a plan. Well, not so much a plan as a hair-brained scheme that just might work. If I could talk Super Agent into going along with it. Big *if* there.

"I thought we settled last night."

"We did." Mostly. "My secret admirer won't make a move with you there."

"No."

"You haven't even heard my idea."

"If it involves leaving you alone without protection to possibly get hurt or killed—no."

"Not *alone* alone. Just hear me out and then you can decide that you really like my idea and go along with it and then this whole thing will be over."

"No."

"Quit being so stubborn."

His gaze tracked to our joined hands and the marks on my wrist. "Haven't you been through enough already?"

Oohhh. The quiet torment in his voice was a punch to the gut. Blinking stinging eyes, I gave his hand a squeeze. "Just listen. If you decide that it's a no-go, then it's a no-go. And I'll do it whatever way you want. Okay?"

He stared out over the dash for a moment then slowly

nodded his head. This was big doings for Super Agent. In a rush I filled him in on my plan for drawing out my stalker. When I finished, Super Agent gave me a quick appraising glance. Heh. I'd surprised him with my cleverness. Maybe not so much cleverness as my ability to be conniving. His second, worried look confirmed the latter.

"I'll call and put things in the works when we get to your place."

Huzzah! He'd gone for it. Although I didn't know why I was so excited. I was the one who was going to have to do all the work.

It was all set up just the way I'd laid it out for Super Agent. Although if I'd known what a control freak he'd be about it all, I would've tried to come up with an entirely different plan. That man would make some child a very good mother one day. We barely had time as it was to get everything together, let alone check, recheck, double and triple recheck, and check yet again.

Stratford's Department Store was open and I was at the Estelle Landers counter as scheduled. Everything had begun here. This was where I'd started to miss things and where Shasta had been killed. It only seemed logical that this would be where things would escalate.

Or I could be totally wrong, as it was looking more and more likely the closer it came to when I'd get off work and nothing had happened. If I didn't count the reporters who pressed their noses to the windows at the front of the store near the counter, trying to get my attention. They'd thinned considerably since the store had reopened, but there were still a few diehards hanging about like vultures picking at the last scraps.

"Sorry," I told Super Agent through the microphone he'd wired me with. "I clock out in five minutes. I was really hoping the Creepy Creeper would've revealed himself by now and we all could've gone home and gotten a beer."

He didn't respond. Communication had only been hooked up one way, which had been fun for about five minutes and then talking dirty to the thin air had gotten kinda boring. Plus Xavier had overheard me at one point and had thought I'd been talking to him. He wished.

Daryl edged around the counter toward me. He always approached me like I was a caged wild tiger and he was doused in *eau de meat.*

"I thought I'd let you know that I have an interview set tonight for a possible replacement for Shasta," he told me, wearing black because it was Friday. "Thought you might want to sit in on it."

"You're not going to waste my time again and then hire the worst possible person for the job, are you?"

He shook his head.

"What time is the interview?"

"Six o'clock." He pointed up. "In the boardroom."

"I'll be there."

Daryl backed away, keeping his eye on me until he bumped into the Shy Kitty counter and had to break eye contact. He scuttled back to his office without a backwards glance.

Lance slid into my line of sight. "Hi there."

"Hey."

He leaned against the counter, posing like the guy in the ad for Gent cologne. "So I was thinking. Me. You. A bottle of Chianti, some takeout, and a DVD at my place."

"That's first your mistake—thinking. Your second was voicing those thoughts."

"Come on." He shifted a little closer and a cloud of Gent cologne crawled up my nose. "It could be fun. Relieve a little stress." He waggled his eyebrows. "If you know what I mean."

I didn't need to hear Super Agent to know that his back

teeth were grinding.

"Yeah. No," I answered. "I'm pretty sure I already have plans to jab my eye out with a hot poker."

He chuckled. "That's what I always liked about you—your sense of humor." His gaze drifted south and his tone turned oily. "But not the only thing. There's a *whole* lot about you to like."

I scrunched up my nose, trying to prevent a sneeze, and pointed to the other side of the cosmetics department. "You can like it from over there with all of your teeth intact."

"Your mouth says one thing, but your body tells me another." He moved even closer, crowding my personal space and pissing me off. "So which should I believe?"

"My fist."

I popped him one. He went down like the stiff, life-sized cardboard cutout of the Gent spokesmodel.

Uh-oh. This wasn't going to go over well with my probation officer.

11

Son of a bitch. I cradled my abused hand. That hurt.

And then holy hell broke loose.

The reporters smelling fresh blood in the water—Lance's, which was spurting from his nose—and a new angle on Shasta's murder, exploded through the doors. Camera flashes burst in the air around me, drawing customers to what was going on.

Dang it. More YourVid clips.

Suddenly there was a lot of noise and a lot of people all around us. I got jostled and bumped back by the crowd that had started to form around Lance, who was out cold. I moved back, desperately needing to get away from all the noise and confusion. Someone shoved a cell phone in my face and blinded me with the flash. I stumbled around, my vision dotted and blurry, right into a body.

A hot and hard body. A body I'd felt before. A body I'd had on top of me, all around me, inside me.

Super Agent.

He wrapped an arm around me and hustled me out of the growing crowd and into the elevator.

"How am I supposed to keep you out of jail when you keep assaulting people on camera?"

I blinked up at him, trying to clear my vision. *"Are you*

laughing at me?"

"You've got quite a right cross there, Knockout. Remind me never to get on your bad side."

"He's had that coming awhile, but da-yam." I shook my hand. "That hurt."

He took my hand in his. "I'll see if I can get you some ice." He placed a kiss on the back of my hand. "Are you all right?"

"I'm clearly not right in the head." I flexed my fingers. "Or in the hand."

"You'll make better mistakes tomorrow."

"I thought so yesterday, but I'm not so sure today."

The elevator doors opened to the first floor. Super Agent guided me toward store security office where he'd been hanging out all day watching me and listening in.

As we entered, one of the security personnel scooted past us. "I've got to go help with crowd control," the guy said. He nudged his chin at me as he left. "Nice hit."

"I have a feeling the guys around this store are going to start giving you a wide berth," Super Agent said.

"You seem awfully pleased about that."

He hitched a shoulder and headed for the door. "Where can I find some ice?"

"You're jealous."

His gaze connected with mine. "You're a beautiful woman, Maggie. Guys are gonna notice. I like it. What I don't like is them forcing you to protect yourself. The ice?"

"Employee lounge. Go back out the way we came and go toward the escalators then hook a left. You'll see the door. The code is 1-2-3-4."

"Are you kidding?"

"Yeah, we're like the Pentagon around here."

"Stay here. I'll be right back."

Alone in the security office I took a moment to look around. I'd been in here once before to collect a reward for catching a customer trying to pass off stolen gift cards.

There was a wall of TV screens with different camera angles all over the store. I sat down in a wheeled office chair and scooted forward to watch Super Agent make his way out of the hallway and onto the sales floor.

Man that dude was sexy. The way he moved, like a panther, all sleek darkness and tightly packed power. My lady parts sat up like begging dogs, panting, tongues lolling. I reached out and touched his image on the monitor. I wished I could be the right kind of girlfriend for him. He deserved better than me. I guessed I was just going to have to work harder at it.

As Super Agent disappeared into the employee lounge, I switched my attention to the melee going on around the Estelle Landers counter. Lance was now sitting up. Tabitha held a cloth to his nose. I hoped it was broken. More people had joined the crowd and there was some jockeying for position.

Xavier was going to be sorry today was his day off. When this hit the news my phone was going to explode. Too bad I didn't have it with me or I could FaceTime him footage from the security cameras. He'd like that.

My gaze tracked to the stockroom where Shasta had been killed. The camera angle on the other door was odd. If you opened the door, it would block you from being seen and then wouldn't pick you up again until you were on the other side of the floor. Whoever rigged that shelving unit had to have known about that discrepancy.

"Hello, Maggie."

I spun around in my seat. I'd been so wrapped up in my conspiracy theories I hadn't heard the door open.

"Hey, Daryl." Oh, crap. He was here to fire me. I could see it in his face. "I'm so sorry about what happened with Lance. I really didn't mean to hit him. If you'd heard—"

"I know what he says about you. And to you. He's a pig."

"So, I'm not in trouble?" I went limp with relief. I really

needed this job. And I suddenly realized how much I really liked it too.

"Oh, you're in trouble," he said, inching closer. "I saw you with that man. Who is he?"

"It's okay. Security knows all about him—"

"No. Who is he to you?"

"He's my boyfriend. I probably should've talked to you—"

"Should've? Of course you should've. You should've broken it off with him when you accepted my gifts." He was close enough now that I could smell the coffee on his breath. "You're mine, Maggie. Only mine."

Ho-ly *creeper*.

I'd worked with this man for almost two years and never thought...never saw. He seemed so harmless. This man with his mousy looks and timidity had killed Shasta. Because of me.

I cut my gaze to the monitors, hoping to see Super Agent on his way back, but the first floor was virtually empty now. The cosmetics department on the second floor was crammed with people. A fight had broken out between some of the reporters. I watched in dawning horror as the remaining first-floor employees filed onto the escalator to the second floor. Super Agent would be my only hope.

"He's not coming," Daryl said, regaining my attention. "I jammed the door. No one's coming. It's just you and me, Maggie. Forever."

He reached out to touch my face. I leaned as far out of his reach as I could and came up against the counter.

"Ouch!" I reached out to touch the twinge in my side as Daryl showed me the syringe in his hand. "What did you...?"

My last coherent thought was that I wouldn't get to make a better mistake than this tomorrow.

I woke up all at once, gasping as though someone had dumped a bucket of cold water over my head. I tried to move but soon realized I was tied to the rolling chair from the security office. Daryl had secured my forearms to the chair arms and my feet were tucked up under me and strapped to the underside of the chair. He'd even bound me around the waist, cutting into my sore ribs. I wasn't gagged so he must not have been too concerned about me screaming my head off.

I was in a bedroom decorated in late-teenaged nerd with posters of half-naked sci-fi movie starlets tacked to the walls. The bedspread had robot-looking soldiers on rocky terrain, gripping space-aged guns. Spaceship models hung from a ceiling dotted with glow-in-the-dark stars configured in an unfamiliar constellation. On the bedside table was a photograph of Daryl and me. I had no memory of when that picture could've been taken.

Oh, wait. No. It was after last year's sales awards ceremony. I'd won second place. Xavier had taken first as he always did. Xav should've been standing on the other side of Daryl but had been cut out of the picture, leaving just Daryl and me. Major creepy ew!

Where in the heck was Super Agent?

Daryl came into the room, stopped just inside the door,

and set down a tray on the dresser covered in…holy freak-out…pictures of me. And not just from the store. Most of them were of me in my everyday life.

"I've imagined you here so many times. To actually have you here now…" He wiped at his eyes. Was he crying? "It's a dream come true."

"Funny. I was thinking this was an alcohol-induced nightmare and any minute now I'm going to wake up with a raging hangover."

"I've always enjoyed your honesty. You say what you think, how you feel. So refreshing."

"Then you're going to appreciate how completely pissed off I am at being kidnapped and tied to this chair."

He turned and picked up a steaming bowl of soup. "I don't expect you to fall in love with me right away. We'll work on it. You'll come to see we're meant to be together."

"If your plan is to keep me tied up in your childhood bedroom until I fall in love with you, then your plan sucks monkey balls. That's never going to happen."

He chuckled. "And so colorful too. I bet you're quite spirited in bed."

"Okay, first of all, eww. Second of all, untie me. Right now."

He looked disappointed in me. "I can't do that. You see, I've been studying Stockholm syndrome and military basic training techniques. It's going to take some time and unfortunately some efforts I'm not completely comfortable with to turn your mind toward me. You're going to love me. Do you understand?"

"Okaayyyy. I was hoping to reason with you, but I see now that your reason has gone on permanent vacation in Crazy Town."

"I'm not crazy. I'm just a man in love."

"It really doesn't matter how long you keep me here, Daryl, or what you do to me. I won't ever love you. I'm in love with someone else who is on his way here right now to rescue me." Hopefully.

He set the soup down and in two long strides was standing in front of me. He raised his hand and smacked me in the face. Hard. "You're in love with me." He hit me again with his other hand. "You love only me. Now." He pulled at the tails of his shirt, straightening it. "How about some soup. You must be hungry."

My cheeks burned and tears filled my eyes. That hobbit-looking son of a bitch was a lot stronger than he looked. He picked up the bowl of soup again and came toward me. I glared up at him through stubborn watery eyes.

He brought the soup-filled spoon to my lips. "Come on, dear. I know you're hungry. You've been out cold for nearly ten hours. Eat."

That long?

My stomach growled and he smiled. "See. Hungry. And I've brought delicious soup for you, my love. Open up for me."

I let him feed me. When he went for a second spoonful I spat the soup at him. His face grew red and I thought for a moment that he was going to hit me again. Instead he splashed the entire steaming bowl of soup at me.

I screamed. It burned like a son of a bitch.

"I'm sorry to have to do that to you, but how else are you going to learn?" He pulled in a breath and straightened his spine. "Apologize to me."

"What?" I sputtered, trying to shake the soup out of my eyes. "I'm not freaking apologizing to you, you jerk. Let me go!"

"In that case, no food for you for the next twenty-four hours. Everything you need, you're going to get from me, do you understand?" He patted his chest. "I'm in control. I decide what happens to you and when. You need me." He reached out a tentative hand and stroked my face with his finger. I didn't try to bite it off. "Remember that the next time I show you a kindness."

He backed away from me toward the door, gathered the tray, and left. He opened the door a second later and turned the light off. At least I couldn't see the photo collage of me anymore.

I shook my head, squeezing my eyes. They burned from the soup and running mascara.

"Daryl!" I waited a beat and then tried again. "Daryl! Help!"

He burst into the room and flipped on the lights. "What is it, sweetheart?"

"Could you wipe my eyes? They burn."

He frowned. "I suppose that would be okay." He plucked a couple of tissues from a box and wiped my eyes. "Better?"

"Yes. Thank you."

He started for the door.

"I have to go to the bathroom."

Panic flittered across his features. "Let me think about this a moment."

"Could you think faster? I'm about to have an accident here." I pressed my thighs together to prove it.

"Okay. Okay. I'll be right back." He left and then came back with a device that looked like it came from one of his video games. "I'm going to untie you. One false move and I'll hit you with this."

"Did you get that in your box of sugary cereal this morning? It's cute."

"No. It's a Taser."

"*Ooohhh.* I'm scared."

I heard a *zap* and every muscle in my body burned like the worst leg cramp ever.

"Are you scared now?" Daryl asked.

No. I was freaking terrified.

All of a sudden the cramping let up and I could move again. This guy was seriously racking up dead-to-me-list points.

"The probes are still in your arm," he informed me. "All I have to do is hit the trigger again and you go down. I'm going to untie you now."

He worked on my feet, disconnecting them from the chair, but he left them tied together. "So you can't run away," he explained.

I rolled my eyes.

"Lean over," he said. He then untied my left arm and retied it behind my back, securing it with rope around my waist. "Sit up." He freed my right arm. "There." He seemed really pleased with himself.

"I have to hop one-armed to the bathroom?"

"I'm going to roll you to the doorway. Then you'll have to hop."

I had to admit this guy was no dummy. I had about a foot and we won't mention how many pounds on him. I could've easily overpowered him.

He wheeled me toward the bathroom and disconnected the Taser probes. "Don't try anything," he warned.

As if I would. At this point I really did have to go to the bathroom and was afraid one more shock would loosen my bladder. So I hopped into the bathroom and did my business. I was just coming out when I heard a loud crash from somewhere in the house.

Daryl grabbed my arm, shoved me into the chair and pushed me into the bathroom, closing and locking the door after us.

"What was—" Darn Daryl tased me again!

He shoved a handkerchief in my mouth and bound my free arm to the chair. "Be quiet," he warned. "Or I'll tase you again."

Like I had a choice? Finally my muscles relaxed again. Every second with Daryl made me hate him more.

"Oh, no," Daryl breathed.

"Maggie!"

Super Agent! I was rescued.

I tried to yell, struggling in my chair to make as much noise as possible. Freaking Daryl tased me *again*. Daryl's wild gaze swung to the rattling door handle.

"I have a gun! I'll shoot her!" Daryl yelled.

Finally in control of my body again, I worked at forcing the cloth out of my mouth. Eureka! "No, he ugh—" The bastard shocked me again! I was really getting sick of that.

Something hit the door, splintering it. Daryl backed away, tripped on the edge of the bathtub and tumbled in. The back of his head hit the tile with a sickening *thunk*.

Freed from the effects of the Taser, I started yelling my head off and didn't stop until I saw Super Agent come through the door.

"How did you know where to find me?" I asked Super Agent while the paramedics did annoying things to me.

I was fine except for the fact that I smelled like chicken noodle soup and had mascara raccoon eyes. It was going to be nothing but waterproof mascara for me from now on.

We were outside of Daryl's house, sitting in the back of an ambulance. Or at least I was. Super Agent leaned against the opening, watching me get poked and prodded. I'd tried to tell him that I was okay, but he wouldn't listen to me. Finally the paramedics finished and declared me fit but recommended an overnight stay at the hospital to make sure. I declined before Super Agent could agree.

Super Agent picked a noodle out of my hair. "Your microphone was still transmitting. That was very clever of you to casually mention being in his childhood bedroom so we knew where to find you. We'd run out of leads."

I'd totally forgotten about the microphone. "Yeah, I'm clever like that."

"Scared twenty years off my life when you screamed and it cut out."

"That would've been the hot soup."

"And when he hit you..." I felt the look in his eyes deep in the pit of my stomach before he turned away and hid it from me.

I was in so much trouble with this man. Trouble in a good, scary way.

"How'd Daryl get me out of the store?" I asked to bring Super Agent's attention back to me. I liked his attention way too much.

"The security cameras caught him wheeling you out on the office chair and right into the parking garage. We knew he'd taken you, but weren't sure of where until you tipped us off."

"Did you see what he had in the bedroom?"

"The photos? Yeah."

"I can't believe that I've known him for almost two years and had no idea what he was really like."

"You never know what will set someone off. He has a history of mental illness, but nothing that would've given anyone a clue as to what he'd been planning to do."

We both turned to watch another set of paramedics wheel Daryl out to a waiting ambulance. Daryl hadn't regained consciousness since he'd hit his head. I tried to drum up some sympathy for him, but all I had was disgust. He'd killed Shasta and kidnapped me. Who knows how long he would've tried and what he would've done to make me love him. I shuddered at the thought.

"Hey." Super Agent took my hand. "You're okay."

"Yeah, I'll live to make better mistakes tomorrow."

"This isn't your fault, Maggie. None of this is on you. You believe that, don't you?"

"Yeah, sure." No. Not really.

"You knocked out another one. You're getting really good at that, Knockout."

"Not my fault. This one's on you."

"Can't say I'm sorry."

"Do you think he'll make it?"

Super Agent shrugged. "I hope so. I'm looking forward to what will happen to him in prison."

"You have a very attractive revenge streak in you. I like it. A lot."

He crossed his arms across his very broad chest, tucking my hand against his heart, and grinned at me. "Oh, yeah? How *much* do you like me?"

Aww, crap. The microphone. He'd heard me tell Daryl that I loved him. Dang technology!

"That's not on tape anywhere, is it? I mean, please tell me it's not going to be used as evidence in Daryl's trial for the whole world to hear."

"Oh, yes. It's recorded."

Dang. I really did have the worst luck.

He leaned forward, brushing his lips across mine. "I love you too, Knockout."

"No duh. I can't think of any other reason why you'd stick around and put up with my crap. It's either that or you're a masochist."

"Maybe it's a little of both."

"Maybe." I grinned up at him. "And that's why I love you."

THE MISADVENTURES OF MAGGIE MAE

Find Me,
MAGGIE

BETH
YARNALL

FIND ME, MAGGIE

Tonight is *the* night that Maggie Mae Castro and her boyfriend, FBI Special Agent Clive Poole, will finally have thoroughly thought-out, all-options-weighed, completely premeditated, totally intentional sex. There's just one little problem. Maggie's twin brother, Miguel, is missing and his pregnant girlfriend begs Maggie to find him.

Having seen Miguel's rap sheet, Clive is sure this is just another stunt designed to get the con artist out of whatever trouble he's gotten himself into. But as Maggie digs deeper, she discovers that Miguel swindled a very scary man out of a very large sum of money.

Maggie strikes a deal with the man Miguel conned—if she brings Miguel back, her brother lives, if the man's henchmen get their hands on him first, all bets are off. The race is on across state lines. But the con has gone on too long, and even Maggie's best finagling might not be enough to convince Miguel to give the money back—or keep the man from killing her twin.

Dedication

To *my* Super Agent, my husband, Mr. Y. for buying in to and supporting every single one of my crazy Lucy and Ethel schemes...including the one where I thought I could write a book.

And to my sister, Sarah Pirch, for being the very best sibling in the world. Thank you, Sarah Sister!

Find Me, MAGGIE

THE MISADVENTURES OF MAGGIE MAE

BETH YARNALL

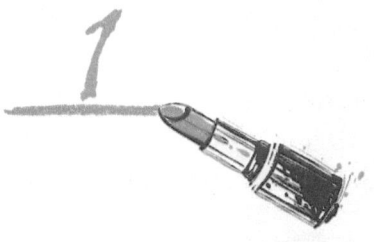

The way a man chewed his food should not have been sexy, but watching Super Agent slide a bite of broccoli between his lips, then slowly withdraw the fork, was hotter than that *Forty-Eight Colors of Carnal* book that may or may not be stuffed under my pillow at this very moment.

He stabbed another piece and I snatched up my wine glass. Really, was it too much to ask for the man to have a flaw? Just one. Or a quirk. I'd even settle for a quirk, like whistling his S's or hoarding sugar packets or something.

FBI Special Agent Clive Poole, aka Super Agent, and I had been dating officially for several months now. I wasn't counting the weeks he'd been my bodyguard and we'd kinda, sorta ripped each other's clothes off while he was assigned by the FBI to protect me from the man-stealing man-slut who'd been out to kill me. I also wasn't counting the time I'd bent the bedposts with him after a traumatic experience, wanting to trade one bad memory for a universe-altering night of screaming his and the Great Almighty's name.

If I counted them, which I wasn't, then I'd have to take a hard look at the huge mutant moth holes in my moral fabric. And I couldn't keep ignoring the raging desire to repeat the experience, right here on top of the pristine white tablecloth, right now with the entire upper crust of Scottsdale as an audience.

"Want more wine?"

I set down the glass I'd been sucking on like a nursing infant to find Super Agent watching me with a mixture of bemusement and concern.

"No," I said to him. "I want to be fully sober when you strip me bare and do things to me that would embarrass a prostitute."

His fork clattered against his plate and bounced onto the floor. "Are you serious?"

He had to ask because I was kinda known to act on impulse and then regret the whole business in the cool light of day. He'd made me promise that the next time we twisted the sheets it would be thoroughly thought-out, all options weighed, completely premeditated, totally intentional sex.

"Yup." I took out my cell phone and showed him how I'd keyed it into my calendar as an hourly event starting in five minutes.

He shot a hand in the air. "Check please!" He shoved his credit card at the waiter as soon as he appeared. "There's an extra twenty in it for you if you run it and come back within sixty seconds."

The waiter snatched the card and took off.

Super Agent eyed me as though I was a magician's trick he was trying to follow. He had that hot-cop thing going on from the top of his cleanly shaven head down to his slightly scuffed wingtips and everywhere in between. I knew for a fact he was packing a lot more than a Glock under his baggy suit. And I was looking forward to being reintroduced to every well-honed, mocha-latte inch of him.

By the time the waiter returned, I had my bag over my shoulder and was already halfway to the door before Super Agent caught up with me.

Placing a hand low on my back he mumbled in my ear, "You might want to call in sick to work tomorrow right now.

What I have planned for you is going to take longer than one night."

"You have a dirty, dirty mouth. I hope you're going to use it for more than boasting."

"Count on it."

Who needed roses and chocolates with a promise like that? Within minutes we were in his car, breaking speed limits. I dug my phone out of my bag and scrolled through my contacts for my new department manager's phone number. Before I could hit *Call*, my phone vibrated.

"Why is *she* calling?" I asked.

"Who?"

"My brother's girlfriend."

I hardly knew her, and it wasn't our birthday for another five months. *Our* as in *mine and Miguel's*. Mine and Miguel's as in twins. Twins as in two people who barely managed to coexist long enough to escape the womb and each other.

"Hello?" I answered.

"Maggie!"

"What's Miguel done now, Alice?" Not that I cared unless you counted the novelty factor. My brother was nothing if not ingenious at the way he could screw up his life.

"He's gone."

"Uh-huh." What did she expect me to do? Miguel went through women like he went through social security numbers.

"Maggie, he's *vanished*."

"Yeah, I got that part." Really, this girl needed to get aboard the Dumped Train and enjoy the ride along with all of Miguel's other castoffs.

"I think something bad's happened to him."

Okay, this wasn't the first time Miguel had left a girl hanging. I'd walked home more times than I could count from places where Miguel was supposed to have picked me up. And this wasn't the first girl I'd talked through Miguel's revolving door. By now I'd memorized the speech.

"Alice, you're a wonderful person." I caught Super Agent's eye-roll out of the corner of my eye. He'd heard me give this speech before. "He doesn't deserve you. One day you'll see that—"

"He didn't dump me. I think he may have been kidnapped...or killed."

And this wasn't the first time I'd heard perfectly sane, articulate and attractive women excuse my brother's rotten behavior with an old-fashioned conspiracy theory.

"He's not kidnapped or murdered. He's just a raging jerk."

Super Agent chuckled.

"He didn't dump me. He loves me. We were making plans for the fu—"

"Miguel doesn't do futures unless we're talking stocks." Alice let out a sob, and my gut twisted for her. I hated Miguel for putting her—and me—through this.

"Please, Maggie."

I gave Super Agent a wistful side-glance and sighed. Miguel was going to pay for this. "What do you want me to do?" I asked Alice.

Super Agent shook his head and flipped a U-turn back toward downtown Scottsdale.

"Come meet me at his apartment and you'll see what I mean," Alice said.

"Fine." Oh! Miguel was *so* going to pay. "We're on our way."

I called Miguel's cell number about eighty times, threatening new and inventive ways I'd hurt him with every message I left. In between I called his friend Eric, who hadn't heart from my brother for a few days. Next I tried my mom. No luck there unless you counted her extracting a promise from me to bring Super Agent over to dinner on Sunday so she could *finally* meet him. I went through Miguel's ex-girlfriends, drinking buddies, and old juvie pals. *Nada.*

We pulled up to Miguel's apartment in a neighborhood way beyond his supposed means, whatever that happened to be this week. The sharp, modern angles of the building and the high-tech, glass-and-steel structure reminded me of my slickly polished brother. It was just like him to surround himself with wealth he didn't come close to possessing.

Super Agent cut the engine. "I'll give you five minutes to sort out Miguel's drama with Alice."

"And then what? You'll throw me over your shoulder and carry me back to your lair?"

"Something like that."

With lines like that was it any wonder I was crazy about him?

Alice opened the door as we came up the steps. "Finally! Come in, come in."

I didn't know how my brother hit a homerun every single time, but he somehow managed to have steadily, increasingly beautiful girlfriends. One after the other they just got more and more stunning. Alice had to be the top of the pinnacle with her gorgeous long red hair and ivory complexion. This was only the second time I'd met her—which was a new record—and I could've sworn she'd gotten more beautiful since the last time I'd seen her.

Super Agent went slack-jawed and glassy-eyed. I hit him in the stomach with the back of my hand. "This is Clive," I told Alice, glaring at my soon-to-be ex-boyfriend. "He'll be sleeping alone tonight."

"Hi." Alice gave Super Agent about a second of her attention, then turned back to me. "I'm so glad you're here, Maggie. I've been so worried."

"Yeah, I got that. When was the last time you saw him?"

"Tuesday morning. We were supposed to meet for dinner after work, but he never showed. The police let me file a missing person report, but there hasn't been any news." Her eyes got all watery, and if it was possible I hated my brother a little more for it.

"Is there anything missing from the apartment?"

"A suitcase and some clothes." She swiped at the tear running down her perfect cheek. "I know what you're thinking."

"No, I don't think you do. Unless you're wondering how Miguel is going to eat and wipe his ass with two broken arms."

She laughed. "You sound just like Miguel."

"That's not going to win you any points with her," Super Agent pointed out to Alice. "When was the last time anyone heard from or saw Miguel?"

"I've pinned it down to five p.m. on Tuesday when he left his office," Alice said. "The last person to see him was the security guard as Miguel walked out the door. He hasn't been seen or heard from since."

The one thing Miguel loved most in this world was being seen and heard from. A slow, insidious slip of dread snaked its way through my chest. Call it twin-tuition, call it a gut feeling, but I believed Alice. Something bad had happened to my brother.

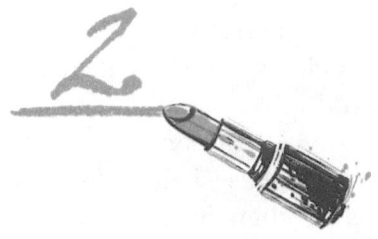

"*Y*ou can't be serious," Super Agent said.

"As serious as the butt-kicking Miguel's going to get when I see him." I'd asked Super Agent for the teeny, tiny favor of putting Miguel on the FBI's missing persons list. I batted my lashes at him. "Pleeeeeease?"

"You really think there's foul play here?" Super Agent obviously didn't.

"Yeah. I kinda do."

"Fine." His gaze dropped to the front of my dress where cleavage ran free. "You're lucky you're so darn sexy."

"And you're going to get *extra* lucking for saying that."

Super Agent moved to the desk in the corner of Miguel's bedroom. We'd promised Alice we'd go through Miguel's things to look for clues she might have missed. I was sorting through Miguel's closet, which smelled faintly of him, reminding me of the last time I'd seen my brother.

He'd stopped by to ask me if he could borrow my car for a few days with some excuse about his tires being too bald to make the long trip he intended to take. I think he knew I'd just washed and gassed it up. As usual I gave in to him. As much as I wanted to, I couldn't blame him for it. There was just something about his smile and the way his gaze moved over your face, taking everything in like a search beam. He'd let his hair grow long, nearly to his shoulders and it had tickled my nose when I'd hugged him goodbye.

"Thanks for the loan of the car, sis."

"Just don't crash it."

He started down my front walk and then turned back. "Do you think I could ask one more favor?"

"You always do."

His laugh was off center, tilting toward self-deprecating. "Yeah, I guess I do." He glanced down at my car key in his hand, then back up at me. His expression bothered me, but I couldn't put a finger on why then or now. Maybe because it was so unlike him as was the favor he was about to ask. "Take care of yourself, okay?"

"Yeah, sure."

The morning sunlight picked up the burnt red in his dark hair and bleached his blue eyes nearly white. I was struck by how much he looked like our dad, and it made my chest hurt.

"I was wondering how your brother managed to get Alice, this house, this life," Super Agent said, drawing my attention back to the here and now. "He's got no discernable income and a rap sheet as long as my right leg. Not to mention the fact that he's a con man. She seems—"

"Too good for him?"

"I was going to say too smart to fall for his B.S."

"You got all that from the optical groping you gave her?"

He stopped rifling through Miguel's desk to glance up at me. "I'm a trained observer. It's my job."

"You're also a dude with working dude parts. At least I assume they're working. Not that I'll get to find out tonight."

"Nah-ah. We have a schedule to keep." He checked his watch. "We're already more than half an hour behind. But we can catch up if we leave soon."

"Like I said, working dude parts."

"I still don't get why you think he's missing. There's

nothing here that would lead to that possibility. No sign of foul play, no ransom note or phone call…nothing."

I pulled my head out of the closet and closed the door. He was right; this was a complete bust. "You're going to think this is nuts."

"Coming from you? No doubt."

"You just got docked an hour, buddy. No make-ups."

"Aww, come on. You've got to admit that you live at the center of a vortex that seems to funnel nothing but trouble your way."

He had a point. I seemed to be a magnet for messed-up tragedy lately. What with getting accused of murdering my ex-Arizona-state-senator boyfriend, nearly being murdered by an FBI-wanted transvestite, being the object of a stalker who'd killed my annoying coworker as some kind of tribute, and being on probation. But I was still docking him the hour for pointing all of that out to me.

"Are you done insulting me?" At his nod I continued. "It's because of the twin thing. I can't really explain it, but it's like there's this other part of me that's not me."

"Like a phantom limb?"

"Yeah, kinda exactly like that. Sometimes I can feel him, like that time when we were ten and he broke his arm. I got a really sharp pain in my arm in nearly the same place at the same time. Same thing happened when we walked in here. I got the feeling that Miguel is in over his head and that he didn't just run, he's hiding. He's in some kind of trouble. I just don't know what it is."

"Okay, so who would know what he's been into lately? Does he have any friends or associates? I can pull his sheet and see who he's been in trouble with before."

"Just like that? You believe me?"

"Yeah."

"Congratulations. You got your hour back."

We finished going through Miguel's condo and even though I found all his hidey-holes—which really impressed

Super Agent—we didn't find anything that would give us a lead on Miguel's whereabouts. We said our goodbyes to a teary-eyed Alice and headed to my apartment across town.

Once there, Super Agent immediately got on the phone and worked his FBI-Special-Agent magic to put Miguel on the FBI's missing persons list and to pull up his rap sheet. He'd been right. Miguel's arrest record was longer than anybody's leg. I had no idea he'd been arrested so many times. Not all of the charges had stuck, which made Super Agent frown. It was kinda cute how he thought every arrest should lead to a conviction, or at the very least some jail time and parole.

Which was pretty ironic considering I was currently on probation without having served any jail time. We almost never discussed my reduced charge of disturbing a crime scene or the fact that I could be sitting in a cell for additional weapons charges. The gun had been registered...just not in my name. The police were such sticklers for that kind of thing. But thanks to my helping the FBI capture the murderer of a state senator *and* an internationally wanted fugitive I'd only gotten two years of probation.

"There is one name that's popped up a few times in connection with Miguel's," Super Agent said.

He was drinking coffee, his feet propped up on my coffee table as if he was prepping for an all-nighter. The thought of what Super Agent could do to me in a whole night made me want to forget my wayward brother and get to the part where he reactivated my dormant lady parts.

"Sergei Levkova."

That name sent a chill through me, blasting away all my other thoughts. Talk about your past coming back to bite you in the behind. Sergei Levkova. I'd briefly thought to call him when I was mentally running through the list of my brother's friends—his name was still in my cell phone. I'd transferred it into three different phones yet I hadn't spoken to him in more than four years. For good reason. I'd put him firmly behind the door marked *Only open in case of severe emergency or complete insanity*.

"Why does that name sound familiar?" Super Agent asked.

Here was the part where I could stare at the ceiling, whistling, or I could come clean.

He grunted. *"That's* why." He turned his laptop so I could see the screen, his FBI-Special-Agent gaze scanning my expression like a laser lie detector. "He shows up on your arrest record too."

Sergei Levkova had contributed to more than my arrest record, but that was something I couldn't discuss with Super Agent.

"We used to hang out," I hedged.

He eyed me some more and I was pretty sure he knew I was hiding something. "Did you know he and Miguel own a business together?"

"No." There was a reason why I didn't keep close tabs on my brother and an even bigger reason why I wouldn't follow whatever he and Sergei had cooked up together.

"Vasili Investments. It looks like it's some kind of investment brokerage firm that boasts high returns. Hmm."

He clacked away on his keyboard some more. I was at the edge of my seat now with the feeling of leaning over my own grave. I sent a frantic, fruitless prayer that he wouldn't dig too far into Sergei or my relationship with him. That was a Pandora's box that should never be reopened. But I knew enough about Super Agent to know he wouldn't stop digging until he had all of his questions answered. And the man *never* ran out of questions.

I popped up out of my seat and tapped my bare wrist. "We're behind schedule. I should've been naked and finding religion an hour ago." Unzipping my dress, I started for my bedroom, hoping some skin would make him forget all about my brother and Sergei. I turned back and looked at him over my bare shoulder. "I'll be in the bedroom assuming the position if you'd like to join me."

My dress slid down the rest of the way to pool at my ankles. I kicked it at him, hitting him mid-chest. He practically threw his computer across the room and leapt off the couch, chasing me until we hit the bed. We landed in a twisted pile of limbs, struggling to rip each other's clothes off. And then he kissed me and I forgot all about Miguel and Sergei.

By the time we were completely naked and rolling around on the bed I couldn't remember my own name. Everything went out of my head except what Super Agent was doing with his hands and oohhhh...his mouth. His glorious, glorious mouth.

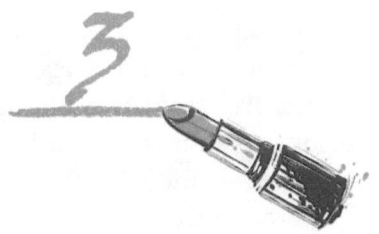

I woke up with Super Agent's warm body pressed against my backside, his arm around me, and his leg over mine. It was like even in sleep he kept me tethered to him as though he was afraid I'd slip away. Which was ironic because that was exactly what I intended to do.

Wiggling like a deranged belly dancer, I was able to work myself free without waking him up. I'd worn him out pretty good so it was little wonder he slept so hard. I managed to find the dress I'd worn to dinner with Super Agent and went into the bathroom to put it on. How I looked was going to be important. I couldn't exactly waltz into the club in my flannel PJs with my hair giving Medusa a run for her money.

Satisfied with how I looked, I tiptoed past a still-snoozing Super Agent with my high heels in hand and made it out of my apartment. I couldn't have come up with an excuse for why I was leaving right after melting the sheets with Super Agent. Not one he'd buy anyway.

The club was in Phoenix, which was only twenty minutes from my Scottsdale apartment, but I sweated the whole way, wondering if Super Agent was going to wake up pissed off and catch up with me. I'd left my cell phone at home on purpose. Mostly because I didn't put it past him to use his FBI-Special-Agent skills to track me like the dog I was. The guilt was killing me, but I couldn't get it out of my head ever since Super Agent had said his name that Sergei was involved in or knew about what my brother was up to.

And I knew just where to find Sergei at one forty-five a.m. I pulled up to the front of EGO, the nightclub Sergei had opened just before we split up, and handed my key to the valet. There was still a line of people waiting to get in even though last call was in fifteen minutes. I sashayed my way to the front and was relieved to find Billy working the door.

He did a double take when he saw me. "Maggie?"

"Yup." I jutted out a hip and propped my hand on it like I still garnered the VIP treatment. "I'm here to see Sergei."

He shook his head, no doubt remembering the way *my* last call with Sergei had gone down, and lifted the velvet rope to let me through. "Good to see you, sexy." I was sure if I turned around I'd catch him checking out my ass, but I was too cool to find out.

The place was pumping as loud and hard as my heart. And it was packed. I didn't get why Sergei would go into business with Miguel when he already had a successful venture like this.

I found Sergei holding court in the VIP section surrounded by women as usual. Another bouncer stood between me and the answer to my brother's whereabouts, but unfortunately I didn't know this one.

"I'm here to see Sergei." I did the hip-jutting thing again, giving Built of Blocks a bored look.

"You and every skirt in club," he said in a thick Russian accent.

"Tell him Maggie's here."

"He know no Maggie."

"Really?" I moved the left strap of my dress and pulled it down to reveal the tattoo I'd had done during my time with Sergei.

Built of Blocks's thick eyebrows jumped up his forehead. "Pardon. I did not know." He motioned me into the VIP lounge.

More than one mistake marked my body, but this tattoo symbolized more than a drunken night gone wrong or a whim I couldn't shake. This one had branded me as Sergei's. He wore its match over *his* heart. They were of his own design and my forever key into his world.

I strolled up to the booth where Sergei lounged with a blonde draped on one side and a brunette on the other and waited for him to notice me. The only way to get Sergei's attention was to not demand it.

He picked up his glass and shot it straight back. That's when he saw me.

"*Myshka,*" he breathed as he set his glass down with a *thunk.*

I'd caught him by surprise. He wouldn't have used his term of endearment for me if I hadn't. His little slip had every head at the table turning in my direction.

"May I have a word?" I asked with more confidence than I felt.

"Leave," he said with a wave of his hands.

They slid out of the booth one at a time, passing me with interested looks and flat-out curiosity. The blonde's jealousy raked over me like claws. I'd have punched her, but I could tell she was just too stupid for me to put out the effort.

"Sit," Sergei told me in his lightly accented English. "Can I get you a drink?"

"No, thank you." I eased into the booth, keeping a respectable distance. "Do you know where Miguel is?"

"I am fine. How are you?"

"Fine. Miguel?"

He made a rude sound and finished off the rest of his drink. We eyeballed each other for a moment. Normally when I run into someone I've gone out with I wonder what I ever saw in him. Not true of Sergei. I remembered exactly why I'd been with him for as long as I had. Setting aside his big, tall, blond, hot Russian-ness, he was charismatic in a way few people are. With him I'd lost all commonsense, the ability to form a single original thought, and my virginity.

"So it's true," he said.

"What?"

"He was smart enough to skip town, but not smart enough to do it without Kostya's money."

"What are you talking about? How would Miguel get ahold of your uncle's money?" Kostya was more than Sergei's uncle, he was as mobbed-up as you could get. If what Sergei was saying was true, my idiot brother didn't just steal from a mobster. He stole from the mob boss himself.

Sergei got the attention of a cocktail waitress and held up two fingers. Shoot. This meant he was about to tell me a story I didn't want to hear.

He ran his dark gaze over me, no doubt taking in what had changed about me while also cataloging what hadn't. He reached out and moved the strap of my dress, revealing the tattoo, *his* tattoo. "You still have it."

"Don't you?"

He lifted his shirt, giving me an eyeful of sculpted abs and *my* tattoo atop his perfect pec. All too soon he covered it back up. "It's good to see you, Maggie. You look good."

"Thank you. So do you."

The waitress deposited our drinks. Sergei picked up his glass, prompting me to do the same. He clinked his against mine.

"To Miguel."

I took a sip of what I knew to be the very best tequila on earth. It had always been nothing but the best for Sergei.

"I helped him start up a new investment firm," Sergei began. "I didn't realize he'd turned it into a Ponzi scheme until after Kostya had invested a large sum of money and Miguel had run off. I started getting phone calls from my uncle three days ago, asking where Miguel and his money were. I love your brother, but he's an idiot. Kostya's looking for him. God help him if he's found." He downed the rest of his drink.

My brother was a flaming idiot to run off with Kostya's money. And he was a dead idiot for sure if Kostya got a hold of him.

"Can you get me in to see your uncle?" I asked.

"Why? Unless you've got two and a half million dollars, you're not going to sway him. He wants his money and to set an example."

"Please?" It was the second time tonight that I'd begged a favor from a man on behalf of my brother. I hated asking for favors and avoided asking for them like you'd avoid your creepy uncle who hugged too long and always wanted you to sit on his lap.

If Kostya didn't kill Miguel I was going to for sure.

Sergei slid out of the booth and held his hand out for me to do the same. "I'll take you to him, but I can't promise you'll get anywhere with him. He's not a charitable man on a good day. And since he lost two and a half mil he's barely civil."

I put my hand in his and stood up. "I'll take my chances."

Sergei elected to ride in my car and have his chauffeured limousine follow us. I'd refused to ride in his limo. I wanted my own wheels should things go south with Kostya.

He directed me to the one restaurant in Phoenix that served authentic Russian cuisine. Ironically, Sergei didn't like Russian food any more than he liked vodka, so he'd never taken me there.

I parked in the back as Sergei instructed. He put his arm around me as we approached the entrance. I let him.

This was some kind of signal to the men at the door that I was allowed to enter. The inside of the restaurant was much fancier than the outside with plush chairs and heavy wooden tables. We found Kostya sitting alone at a table with a laptop open in front of him.

"*Dyadya,*" Sergei said, drawing the old man's attention.

I'd met Kostya several times before when Sergei and I were together, so he recognized me. He said something in Russian to Sergei, and Sergei answered him back the same way. The old man shook his head sadly.

"Sit," Kostya instructed. "Not you," he told Sergei. "The pretty one. You give this to Anya." He held out an envelope to Sergei. "And don't come back until I call for you." He turned to me when Sergei was out of earshot. "You have news of your brother and my money?"

"No. If I knew where he was I would've dragged his behind in here and made him give it back to you."

"I don't like being made a fool of." He leaned closer and lowered his voice. "Neither does my nephew."

I was pretty sure he was talking about more than Sergei's business venture with Miguel. Sergei and I had some unfinished business that as far as I was concerned could stay unfinished.

"And I don't like having an idiot for a brother. Looks bad on my resume."

"Ha! Pretty *and* funny. I like you. Always did."

"Don't forget smart. I'll do what I can to get him back here…with your money."

He stared at me for a moment. "What makes you think you can convince him to do this?"

"I have my ways. I'll make you a deal: If I find my brother and bring him back here with your money, you don't kill him."

"And if I find him first?"

"Then I'll have a dead idiot for a brother."

He barked out another laugh, smacking his palm on the

table and making his computer jump. "I like you *a lot*. You have guts. I'll make that deal with you. On one condition."

I never thought I'd get this far with the old man. He could slap whatever condition he wanted on the deal. "What's that?"

"Sergei goes with you."

Except that one.

I thought about the FBI Special Agent lying naked in my bed right now and it was on the tip of my tongue to tell Kostya no, no way in hell. But then I thought about my mother and how she'd blame me for Miguel's death even though I'd have nothing to do with it. Not to mention the fact that I'd also have a dead brother. On the other side was a possible road trip with Sergei and a *very* pissed-off boyfriend.

"That won't work for me," I told him. "Sergei could tip you off." There. Logic.

"Are you calling me a cheat?"

Shoot. Not very well-thought-out logic. "Not you. Sergei."

"You know better."

Kostya didn't know his nephew like I did. Sergei would cheat a nun out of her scriptures if it made him money. "I don't think it would be a good idea if we spent time together."

"That's my deal. Take it or leave it."

Frick. Frack. Frikity frack!

As I shook Kostya's hand, sealing the deal, I cursed my stupid brother and his stupid greed. Kostya would get his money back, but my brother's life was still up in the air. I'd make darn sure Kostya didn't get his hands on Miguel...so I could kill him myself.

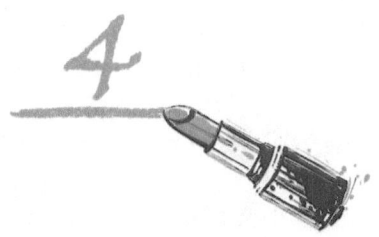

4

I sneaked back into my apartment like a teenager breaking curfew. It was dead quiet. I kicked off my shoes and unzipped my dress just inside the door, then I tossed the dress down where I'd dropped it earlier when I'd seduced Super Agent and tiptoed down the hall. I could just make out Super Agent's form in the bed. I'd done it!

The light clicked on. Super Agent sat up in bed wearing a look I'd never seen before. A very scary look.

"*Where have you been?*"

At this rate my brother was going to cost me more than a few lost hours of sleep. I took off the rest of my clothes, hoping to distract him again. No such luck.

"Maggie," he warned.

I sighed and slipped into bed next to him. "Out looking for Miguel."

"Is there a reason you didn't take your cell phone?"

"I forgot?"

"Where did you go?"

"I went to see the man whose money Miguel absconded with."

He tilted his head to the side. "What?"

"That investment thing Miguel had going? Turns out it was some kind of Ponzi scheme he cooked up. Miguel decided to take off with the money. Two and a half mil and then some."

"Who was this man you went to see?"

"Kostya Levkova."

"Uncle of Sergei Levkova and reputed mob boss...that Kostya Levkova?"

"That's the one." Wait. How did he...? "How long have you been awake?"

"Since you wiggled out of my arms and snuck out the front door."

Frick. Frack. Frickin frack! I was clearly way out of practice. Back in the day I would've been in and out with no one the wiser. Ugh. I could only guess what Super Agent had been up to while I was gone. His favorite thing...research.

"You want to tell me about your *real* relationship with Sergei Levkova? The two of you didn't just hang out, did you?"

"We did some of that." In between a little breaking and entering and having sex like a couple of coked-up rabbits.

His gaze dropped to my chest, and I was pretty sure he wasn't checking out my rack. "And getting matching tattoos."

"Yeah, there was some of that too. You really want to hear about me and another guy?"

"I really don't like being lied to."

I went up to my knees and pointed at him. "And I really don't like being accused of something I didn't do." Technically.

He flipped the covers back, got out of bed (naked!) and started gathering his clothes.

"Where are you going?"

He answered without looking at me. "Home."

"Fine. You want to hear all about me and Sergei?"

I climbed off the bed and went to my dresser, the one with the special drawer. I unlatched the mechanism to the secret compartment and pulled out an envelope. Stomping all the way over to where Super Agent stood with his clothes bundle in his arms, I grew more and more furious.

There were very few things Super Agent didn't know about me. He'd had me under surveillance for nearly a year while he investigated my dead senator ex-boyfriend. What wasn't in my FBI file he got to fill in by watching me day in and day out. This envelope contained one of the few things almost no one knew. My most precious and painful mistake.

I thrust the envelope at him with a look that dared him to take it this one step too far. There was no going back from this. He'd have stripped me bare of the most private parts of my life. We'd been on uneven ground from the start. This would put us miles apart. Miles I wasn't sure we could ever cross.

"Well?" I challenged. "Aren't you going to take it?"

He put his palm up, pushing the envelope back at me. "Don't."

"Don't what? You aren't just accusing me of lying. What else are you accusing me of? Go on. Say it."

"What am I supposed to think when you sneak out in the middle of the night to see your ex-boyfriend?"

"Right. Because that's my MO. Sneaking off to see other men still stinking of sex and you." It was kinda true in this case, but not the way he was making it out to be.

"Maggie." He dropped his clothes and came toward me. "I'm sorry. I just can't stand the thought of you with anyone else."

Then he was really going to hate the little road trip I was about to take with Sergei.

"You either trust me or you don't. Which is it?"

"I trust you."

I glared at him for another minute before turning around and putting the envelope back. It was best left there hidden away in the dark where I didn't have to think about it. I could feel his eyes on me as I climbed back into bed and turned away on my side. After a moment I felt the bed dip on the other side and the light went out.

Super Agent came up behind me and put his arm around me (still naked!). "I'm sorry." He nuzzled my neck.

"If you think you're getting any more tonight you're as crazy as my Aunt Daisy."

He chuckled. "I won't push my luck."

"That's the smartest thing you've said since I came home."

Super Agent kissed me goodbye the next morning, putting a little extra effort into it, which meant that by the time he was done I was swaying like a drunken sailor on deck during a massive storm.

"Wow" was all I could manage.

"I'll see you tonight." He opened the door to go off to work, but that's as far as he got. "What the hell are you doing here?"

I peeked around Super Agent's large frame to see who had made him go from zero to pissed-off in three-point-four seconds. For the love of all that's fair!

Sergei.

The two squared off like a couple of bucks in mating season. I rolled my eyes at them and went in search of coffee. If it had been seven p.m. instead of a.m. I would've hit the hard stuff. It was way too early to deal with the waves of testosterone that pumped off of the two of them.

"Who the hell are you?" Sergei shot back.

"Let him in, Clive," I told Super Agent.

Super Agent opened the door wider and waved Sergei in. They stood nearly eye-to-eye. While Super Agent had about thirty pounds of muscle on him, Sergei matched it in attitude. Super Agent closed the door but didn't leave. He just stood there like a bouncer with his arms crossed.

This was going to be fun.

I made the introductions like we were at a cotillion or something equally civilized.

"What are you doing here?" I asked Sergei.

Sergei looked from me to Super Agent in his wrinkled suit and back again. It wasn't too difficult for him to figure out what was going on here what with me still in my robe and a major case of bed-head. The flicker of hurt in his eyes didn't surprise me, but it gave me a sharp pain in the chest all the same.

"I have a lead on Miguel," Sergei finally said.

Super Agent stirred. "So give it to her and leave."

"That's not the deal."

Darn Kostya and his darn deal!

"What deal?" Super Agent asked.

Sergei lifted a brow. "You don't confide in him?"

"We were a little *busy*," I shot back.

A corner of Super Agent's mouth twitched.

Sergei got that look in his eye again. I knew it wasn't fair of me to take my frustrations with Miguel and Kostya out on Sergei, but if we were going to do this thing I wanted to set some boundaries with him right off the bat.

I filled Super Agent in on the bargain I'd made with Kostya. Needless to say he was less than thrilled.

"No," he said before I was even finished.

Sergei settled on the sofa for a ringside seat to my argument with Super Agent. I motioned for Super Agent to join me in the kitchen out of earshot.

"What happened to all that trust you had in me last night?" I whispered to Super Agent.

"I trust you, not him."

"I'm doing this." I wrapped my arms around his neck and leaned in. "I can't let anything happen to my brother. Please understand."

He brought me in closer, smoothing his hands up my back. "You know I'm going to have to work this too."

"You already are."

"Are you going to give me the lead he says he's got?"

"Depends on if it's a good one or not."

"You frustrate me."

"You like it."

He touched his forehead to mine. "I like it too much. Be careful."

"I will." I put a hand to his cheek. "I love you."

"I love you too." And then he kissed me long and deep, going all out to prove a point to Sergei, who had clicked the TV on as soon as I put my arms around Super Agent. "I don't trust him," he said again when he finally let me up for air.

"I don't either, but I do know that he'd never hurt me." At least not physically.

To say Sergei's and my relationship had been complicated was an understatement. There'd been a lot of pain that hadn't ended when we had. I could almost feel the envelope through the wall to my bedroom. It contained the one thread I couldn't cut that would always tie me to Sergei.

"Miguel hasn't used his credit cards so wherever he is, he's using cash," Super Agent said.

"Thanks for the info."

I walked Super Agent to the door and he gave me another kiss that had me fanning myself as I closed it after him.

"Sleeping with a cop," Sergei said, clicking the TV off. "You can't be that desperate."

Sergei and I had both honed the skill of police-spotting at an early age.

"He's a Special Agent with the FBI."

"A Fed? Kostya's not going to be happy about this."

"Kostya can kiss my shapely behind. He made this deal. If he had more conditions then he should've been upfront about them. Besides, who's going to tell him?" I glared at

Sergei, daring him to snitch.

"He'll find out one way or another."

"Not my problem."

My cell phone rang. Alice. I really didn't have time to hold her hand.

"Hi, Alice."

"Have you found him yet?"

"No, but I'm working on it."

"I really need you to find him, Maggie."

"I'll do my best."

"No. I mean I *really* need you to find him... I'm pregnant."

I felt around for the barstool and sat down. "*What?*"

"You're going to be an aunt."

The joy in her voice made me unreasonably angry. How could Miguel have done this? I wished I shared her happiness. Best-case scenario here would be Miguel in prison, worst case...well, it would be *the worst* possible case. What kind of father could he possibly be?

"Congratulations," I muttered. "I gotta go. Bye."

I clicked *End Call* and turned to Sergei. "We need to find my jerk of a brother. Now. What's your lead?"

"It's not so much a lead as a hunch. A few months back we were shooting the breeze and he mentioned this place in Oregon. Coo or Coop something—"

"Oh, my God. I can't believe I'm related to him sometimes."

"You know the place?"

"Coos Bay. Our dad took us up there to camp for his yearly forced visitation when we were kids. It makes sense. Clive says Miguel hasn't used his credit cards."

"It'll be a long drive."

"Let's make sure he's there before we hop in the car, Thelma."

I brought up the campground we used to go to on my computer and called them. If Miguel was dumb enough to hide at the campground then he was probably dumb enough to use his usual alias.

"Hi. I wanted to check and make sure my husband made it to your campground. He's not answering his cell and... Uh-huh. Michael Cast. Thank you so much. It's good to know he's alive so I can kill him." I hung up the phone and rolled my eyes at my stupid brother's complete and total stupidity. "He's there," I told Sergei. "Looks like we're going north."

5

Sergei and I flew to Eugene, Oregon, then rented a car to drive the rest of the way. We could've flown into a smaller airport within ten miles of Coos Bay, but besides the expense—which Sergei had offered to pay—we couldn't give Kostya too big a clue as to where we were headed. Landing in Oregon was bad enough. We didn't need to give him a road map with a big red arrow on it— Lookie! Here he is!

According to Super Agent, the FBI had gotten wind of Miguel's little "investment" company shortly before he'd skipped town. Now that he was on the run they were more eager than ever to find him. We now had a three-way race. Actually a three-and-a-half-way race since I'd made a little side deal with Super Agent as backup insurance before boarding the plane with Sergei. I honestly didn't care if the FBI beat us to Miguel as long as Kostya didn't.

"We're going to have to pay cash from here on out," Sergei said as we climbed into our rental car. "And pop the batteries out of our cell phones so they can't be tracked."

We'd kept up only the most necessary communication. Eye contact was brief and awkward. I was having a really difficult time being around him again. Too many memories, too much to avoid talking about.

Sergei pulled out a paper map and handed it to me.

"Old school."

I unfolded the map, nearly clocking him in the jaw and causing him to crash. "Sorry."

"No problem."

Like I said, minimal communication.

I found where we needed to go and guided him to the freeway. The silence sat between us like an overweight third passenger. I stared out the window, fiddled with the radio, filed my nails, and tried to sleep—anything to relieve the tension.

I finally couldn't take it anymore. "Why did Kostya insist on you coming with me?"

"He has this crazy notion that I'm still in love with you. He thought it would be some kind of romantic reunion."

I snorted. "He still reads romance novels?"

"All the time."

"You're not though, right?"

Now it was his turn to scoff. "What do you think?"

Honestly, I had no idea. I hoped not. This trip was uncomfortable enough without that complication. "Maybe if he wasn't so busy matchmaking he wouldn't have lost his money to my brother."

"Maybe."

"Your club seems to be doing well."

"It is." He tapped the steering wheel in time with the music on the radio. "You in love with that Fed?"

"Yeah."

"You always did have rotten taste in guys."

"You included?"

"I'm the one exception."

I laughed, but it wasn't very convincing. "Sure you are."

"Why'd you keep it?"

His question caught me by the throat. "What?"

"The tattoo."

I hitched a shoulder, trying to hide my overreaction. "I didn't want to forget."

And that was the God's honest truth. I didn't ever want to forget the catalyst that had made me finally wake the heck up and leave Sergei. The sound of the shots. The look on my best friend Bea's face when the bullet hit her square in the chest. The bullet that had been meant for Sergei. I would've been standing next to him, but I'd gone back to the car to get something, leaving Bea to take the bullet for me.

"Why did you keep your tattoo?" I asked.

"Wouldn't have mattered if I removed it. Can't erase memories with a laser."

"No. You can't."

"Do you ever wonder...?" He shook his head. "Never mind. It doesn't matter."

"No. I don't. The dreams are bad enough."

"Yeah."

I glanced over at him. He dreamed too?

"I was there, *myshka*," he said quietly. "I was there."

Turning away, I hid the tears that suddenly sprang up out of nowhere. I hated to cry. Especially about things I couldn't change.

He reached over and clasped my hand. It had been so long since we'd touched. I'd almost forgotten how it felt. It was more than ironic that I should find comfort from the person who'd caused so much of my pain. Maybe he wasn't the only one with unresolved feelings.

Freaking Kostya and his freaking romance novels.

We drove in silence the rest of the way. I was afraid anything I thought to say would just lead us back to the thing neither one of us wanted to talk about. So I kept conversation to turn-by-turn directions. He never let go of my hand.

After what felt like forever, but was really a little over two hours, we pulled into Coos Bay. I'd forgotten what a picturesque town it was. If I had been with anyone else for any other reason I would've wanted to take a walk on the boardwalk and watch the sunset. But I wasn't here to enjoy myself. I was here to find my brother.

I directed Sergei to the Sunset Bay State Park. The sun lay low in the sky, dipping its bottom edge into the Pacific Ocean and sending out fragile pinks, oranges and yellows across the water. I wished Super Agent were here to see this. We hadn't even taken a vacation together yet. This felt a lot like cheating on him for some reason, making me more uncomfortable than ever.

I slid my hand from Sergei's, disguising the gesture by pointing out the campground office. "Let's find out which cabin he's in."

We climbed out of the car and headed toward the entrance. When we got inside, a young woman greeted us with a chirpy hello. I hung back and let Sergei handle this. Back in the day when we'd run cons of our own, we had a deal that I would handle the men and he'd handle the ladies. It seemed that part of our past wasn't so past tense.

Sergei leaned on the counter, amping up his megawatt smile and his accent. "Hi. I'm Sergei. My sister Maggie and I are hoping you can help us. We're looking for our brother, Michael Cast. He wanted us to come up and hang out, but he's not answering his cell and he didn't tell us which cabin he was in."

"Oh." She blushed. "I'm not really supposed to give that kind of information out."

Sergei leaned a little closer and lowered his voice. "I wouldn't want to get you in any trouble."

"I'd help you if I could."

"I know you would. We'll just keep trying his cell." He started to go and then turned back around, cranking up the charm to blinding. "If I leave without saying anything I know I'll regret it later so... You're very pretty." He lowered his voice to where I could barely hear. "I swore I wouldn't get involved so soon after my girlfriend cheated..." He worked up the perfect expression, a combination of sadness yet hopefulness. "But I feel like we have a connection."

The girl nodded and leaned a little closer, her eyes wide, her lips parted. He had her eating out of his hand now. This is why we'd been so successful.

"Would you join me for a walk later…after you get off work?" Sergei said. "Or we could just sit and talk right there on the porch." He jabbed a finger over his shoulder. "If we ever get a hold of our brother," he added for emphasis. Man he was good.

The girl bit her lip. I held my breath.

"I suppose it wouldn't hurt…" She looked through her records. "He's in cabin 23."

"What time do you get off work?"

"Seven."

"I'll see you at six fifty-nine." He traced a finger along her jaw line, making her shudder. "Beautiful."

We started to leave, but the girl brought our attention back to her. "My name's Rebecca."

"Rebecca…" Sergei said her name like a blessing, giving her one last smoldering look before we left.

We climbed back into the car. I didn't feel good about the way we'd tricked that girl, getting her hopes up. That wasn't the person I was anymore…or at least the person I was trying to be.

Sergei turned to me, his smile triumphant. "Just like old times."

"Yeah. Just like them."

He started the car and put it in drive. "I miss having you as my partner."

I didn't comment. There might have been a few things I missed about Sergei, but tricking innocent people wasn't one of them.

We wove our way through the campground, looking for Miguel's cabin. Sergei drove past it and then turned around, parking a couple of cabins away. There were too many cars around cabin 23. I had a real bad feeling about this.

We climbed out of the car and slipped between two other cabins, heading around the back. The shotgun-style cabins were long and narrow with a living room that led to a bedroom that led to the kitchen at the back. Each had a front and back door with mere feet separating one cabin from the other.

It freaked me out more than a little how Sergei and I had fallen into our old partnership roles without communicating. Careful not to make any sound, we ducked under the windowed backdoors of the other cabins. When we got to Miguel's cabin, Sergei dipped below the window in the door and came up on the other side. We slowly and carefully crouched low and peered up into the window.

For heaven's sake! When was I going to catch a break?

The bulky outline of Kostya's number-one goon, Ivan, filled most of the window. I could just make out Miguel's profile as he sat tied to a chair, his chin on his chest. There was another guy, but I couldn't tell who it was. Probably another of Kostya's men. I closed my eyes and slid down the door. We were too late.

Sergei leaned against my shoulder and whispered, "The deal was for whoever brought Miguel back to Kostya, not for who got to him first."

That was true. "We can steal him back."

"Yup."

We crouch-walked back the way we'd come and climbed into the car.

"So what's the plan?" I asked.

"We'll wait here and see where they take him. And look for an opportunity to snatch him back."

That didn't seem like much of a plan. In fact it was a completely chicken plan and totally unlike Sergei. Either he was losing his touch or there was something else going on here, like maybe he'd tipped off Kostya. Or else he was running his own end game that neither Kostya nor I knew about. If I had to lay down money I'd put it on the latter.

Sergei, like Miguel, always worked his own angle and had at least two contingency plans in reserve.

My fingers itched to pop my battery back in my phone and call Super Agent. He'd swarm the place and arrest Kostya's goons and Miguel. The only wrench in that plan was that I didn't know what orders Kostya had given his guys. They might just shoot Miguel to satisfy Kostya's revenge before trying to escape.

"What makes you think they're going to move him *alive*?" I asked, spitting out a piece of fingernail. I'd chewed my nails to nubs over my idiotic brother. Waiting was not my best skill.

"Kostya won't kill him until he sees him and says what he needs to say. It's an old- school kind of thing that's going to work in our favor."

"They could just pack him onto a plane and we'll never get our chance."

He made a scoffing noise. "It would be really hard to explain a tied-up man to airline staff if you're not the police, and Kostya's too cheap to pay for private. They'll drive him back down to Arizona."

What he said had a certain kind of logic to it—frustrating and aggravating logic—but logic nonetheless.

It was full dark before anything stirred near cabin 23. But it wasn't the Hail Mary we needed. It was more like the makings of complete and total cluster-up.

*H*elpful Rebecca of the front office strolled up to the cabin, no doubt wondering why Sergei hadn't shown for their little get-to-know-you-so-I-can-get-in-your-pants chat.

I punched Sergei in the arm. "Your girlfriend is here looking for you, lover. You'd better go head her off before she knocks—shoo! Too late. Actually...this might be the break we've been waiting for. You go talk to Rebecca and distract Ivan. I'll see if I can go in through the back and sneak Miguel out."

He slipped a knife out of his boot. "Need this?"

I pulled my much-bigger knife out of my bra and rolled my eyes at him. Switching off the overhead light, I opened the car door, then ran behind the cabins, ducking under windows, until I got to Miguel's cabin. Slipping the lock pick into the keyhole I began working on the lock. Bingo.

"Rebecca!" Sergei shouted.

I heard her say something in return. Ivan said something I couldn't understand.

This was my cue. I kept low as I slowly opened the back door. Sergei was talking to Ivan and the other goon in Russian at the front of the cabin, probably feeding them some B.S. line. I found Miguel tied to a chair in the kitchen.

His head popped up when he saw me, surprise parting

his lips, but he was smart enough not to make a sound. I quickly cut his bonds and then signaled for him to follow me back out the way I'd come. He nearly fell on his face when he tried to stand up.

"My legs are asleep," he whispered.

I checked over my shoulder. Sergei still had them occupied out front, but not for much longer. Grabbing Miguel's arm, I slung it around my neck and helped him stand. We made slow progress, but soon we were behind the cabins, headed for the car.

"Faster," I told him in a low voice. "We're almost there."

I was grateful for the darkness as I shoved Miguel into the backseat and then went around to the driver's side. Sergei had left the keys so I could grab Miguel and then swing around front to pick him up.

"Stay down," I told Miguel as I started the car. "I'll tell you when to get up."

"Thank God you got here when you did. Kostya was due any minute."

Sure enough, just as we passed cabin number 23 and the little group standing around out front, we also passed Kostya in a car headed in the opposite direction.

I hit the accelerator, skidding around a corner and out the front gate of the campground. I was going so fast I almost missed the look of shock on Sergei's face as I waved goodbye. This was not part of our pact. We always met up if separated. My wave let him know that I was leaving his double-crossing ass here with Rebecca and his crazy-assed uncle.

By the time I hit the highway, we were going about forty miles an hour above the speed limit. I was sure Kostya and his goons had seen me, so I wanted to put as much distance between us as possible.

Miguel sat up and clicked his seatbelt on. "That was awesome, sis. Just like the old da—hey!"

I reached back and hit him. I kept on hitting him as

best as I could with one hand on the wheel, nearly swerving into the next lane. "That was not awesome." *Slap.* "I can't believe I'm related to you." *Slap, slap.* "You're such an idiot." *Slap, slap, slap.*

He tried to dodge me, but he was so big I landed more smacks than I missed.

"Jesus, stop! Dang it, Maggie. You're as bad as Mom."

That earned him three more whacks. "You think I wanted to fly up here to save your sorry ass with Sergei as a chaperone? I'm out of vacation days so this is coming out of my sick pay, and I was planning on using them for a trip to Mexico. I can't believe you were dumb enough to cheat Kostya out of two and a half million freakin' dollars. What were you thinking?" I hit him once more to drive the message home.

"I didn't take Kostya's money."

"Right. And I'm not Queen of My-Brother's-a-Frickin'-Idiot-Ville."

"I swear to God, Maggie. I didn't steal his money. Sergei did."

And suddenly it all made sense. Sergei must've said something to Kostya back at the restaurant to get himself in on the hunt for Miguel and then played it off as Kostya's romantic side. Add to it his willingness to help me find Miguel and get him away from Kostya's goons. There was only one reason why. He wanted to find out how much Miguel knew and then he'd get rid of Miguel himself.

"Are you being straight with me? Because *I* swear to God, Miguel, that if you're lying to me I'm going to mule-kick your nuts so far up into your head they'll replace your eyeballs."

He grabbed his crotch and crossed his legs defensively.

"I don't like being played...by you or Kostya or Sergei. Now tell me what happened with Kostya's money before I turn this car around and deliver you right back into his lap."

Miguel laid it all out. Sergei was the one behind the Ponzi scheme. He'd gotten his uncle to invest a butt-load of cash and then fixed the books so it looked like Miguel had taken off with the money.

"Only I'm smarter than Sergei thinks," Miguel said.

I highly doubted that. Sergei had counted on the fact that Miguel had built a reputation for screwed-up deals and less-than-honest business practices. From the beginning I'd wondered why Sergei would go into business with my brother. Now I knew. He needed a fall guy and Miguel was practically perfect in every single way.

My gut burned, thinking about how I'd nearly broken down in front of Sergei. He'd played on my sympathies and sentimentality. And I'd let him. There was more than one idiotic Castro sibling in this car.

"I found the offshore bank account where Sergei hid the money," Miguel continued. "I have the account number. He doesn't know I found it. I took off, trying to buy some time so I could hack into the bank account and get Kostya's money back. Then Ivan and Andrei showed up and I was out of time."

"Instead of going to the police?" I couldn't believe this guy had procreated. Just what the world needed…more Miguels. I pulled the car over. "Get in the front seat."

"You're not going to drive off as soon as I get out of the car, are you?"

"You have ten seconds…ten…nine…"

He quickly climbed out of the back and into the front and we were once again speeding down the highway. I continued up Highway 101 to the 5 Freeway heading north back up to Eugene and the airport. As everyone would expect.

And then it hit me.

Dang it. I resisted the urge to smack myself in the forehead. I was so dumb. I'd played right into Sergei's scheme.

My escape with Miguel had gone off without a hitch. Pretty much right on cue. Looking back, I realized everything that had happened since I'd approached Sergei's club had fallen together almost as though things were going according to plan. Sergei had been too complicit and too cooperative from the start, helping me find Miguel. He wasn't exactly the helpful sort. I'd been so focused on my own feelings in that club that I hadn't seen what was right in front of me. Sergei hadn't been surprised. He'd been triumphant. I'd come to him exactly the way he'd planned.

The mess Miguel and I were in was so much deeper than I'd imagined. Whatever Sergei's end game was, I was somehow a part of it. I needed to come up with something to throw a major wrench in the works.

"Why didn't you go to the police?" I asked again. This all could've been avoided if he'd just gone to the cops in the first place.

"Why would I go to the police?"

I punched him in the arm. "To save yourself from being killed, ya dumbass."

"Hey! I didn't move up here just so you could get in a better shot."

"You have no idea what I've been through in the last two days because of you. I went to see Sergei, for God's sake." My vision got all watery, which pissed me off even more. "And you could've been killed."

"Aw, jeez, Maggie. You're not going to cry, are you? Shoot. I'm sorry." He put his arm around me and laid his head on my shoulder.

I swiped at my eyes, trying to see the road. It hadn't really hit me until this moment—with him here safe beside me—just how bad things could've turned out, how bad they could still be. And it was more than the blame my mother would crash down on top of my head. I'd miss the big dumb oaf.

"I thought I could work things out on my own," he said

quietly. "My name's on all the documents. This was supposed to be my big break into legit business. I'd even gotten a couple of clients on my own. Of course Sergei took all their money too so all that's down the crapper." His sigh was full of regret and defeat. "Even if we can get the money back, the cops are already looking at me, aren't they?"

"Yeah."

"There's no way to get that Fed you're sleeping with to take care of that for me, is there?"

"He might've been able to help if you'd gone to him instead of running off. Seriously, dude. *What were you thinking?*"

He sat up in his seat. "I wasn't."

"Well then thank God one of us finally is."

Before I'd left with Sergei, I'd filled Super Agent in on our plan to get Miguel back. He'd added a twist—I was supposed to meet agents from the Portland FBI office in Eugene and deliver Miguel. But with my sudden realization about Sergei I knew I couldn't follow Super Agent's plan exactly the way he'd laid it out. Knowing how Sergei's mind worked, I had no doubt he'd planted some kind of listening device in my apartment. It's what I would've done.

And if he had indeed bugged my apartment, he not only knew about Super Agent's plan, he knew I'd planned to double-cross him from the start. Which meant he probably had guys in position to nab us before we could get to the outskirts of Eugene. I was going to have to think way outside the box to stay one step ahead of Sergei and still deliver Miguel to Super Agent as promised.

The one thing that had driven Sergei nuts when we were together was his inability to control and predict me.

He was going to freaking *hate* what I was about to do next.

I pulled off the freeway and into a busy shopping center.

"Get out," I told Miguel. "And pick out a new car for

us." I was sure Sergei had put some kind of tracking device on this one. It was what I would've done.

My brother was a genius at a few things. Breaking into and hot-wiring cars was one of them. And also, apparently, knocking up his girlfriend. He was going to be in for a shock when he finally talked to Alice.

He chose an older-model Ford and worked his magic. I said goodbye to my probation. Jacking a car would get me a cell right alongside my brother. There was no way Super Agent could gloss this one over, especially since I was no longer following his plan. And grand theft auto hadn't ever been part of our deal. I was looking at time for this for sure, plus the suspended eight-month sentence for that other little thing I'd done that had gotten me probation in the first place.

But I'd rescued my brother from Kostya and Sergei. He was alive. I'd do that and more for him. Sheesh. The things I did for my family.

In less than five minutes we were back on the freeway, this time headed south toward California. I'd dumped out my purse and selected a few things to take with me, like my lipstick, ID, a credit card and all my cash. That was me, traveling light and avoiding capture. Dang it! I really liked that purse too.

The FBI was dying to know what Miguel knew about Kostya. Super Agent was going to get a big ole hard-on when he heard about Sergei's involvement...and the bank account with all that lovely Ponzi cash in it. He might just sport enough wood to try to broker a deal for Miguel.

But I wasn't about to tell Miguel any of this. He'd go along a lot easier with the crap scared out of him than if he went into it thinking everything would be smoothed over for him.

We wouldn't be in the clear until I handed over Miguel to the FBI. If I could ever get him delivered. The only thing that would've made this trip worse was if my mother was in the car with us. I counted that as the one of the two things that had gone right for me this week. The other being finally getting to see Super Agent naked again. Naked!

It was a good thing I had such excellent recall because it was looking more and more likely that the only thing I'd have of Super Agent was a memory.

The thing about being on the run is that you're always looking over your shoulder when you should be paying attention to where you're headed. We'd managed to put a few hundred miles between the head of the Russian mob and us, but it was getting late and both Miguel and I were exhausted.

We found a No-Tell Motel just outside of Redding, California and since the desk clerk was male, I was up to bat.

I yanked my shirt down in front and readjusted my boobs so they were spilling out the V-neck. Letting my hair down from its ponytail, I shook it out. A little lipstick and I was good to go.

I put an extra swing in my step as I came through the door. "Hi."

The clerk did a jerky double take then cracked a stained, gap-toothed smile to rival any meth addict's. "Hellooooo."

"I need a room. A double. But..." I arched my back a little, leaning forward to rest my breasts on the countertop. "I don't have any ID. Is that going to be a problem?"

His gaze zeroed in on Wanda and Wendy, giving them a visual groping I could almost feel. "Do you, um, have a credit card?"

I tried to sound sad, putting out my bottom lip a little. "No."

"Well, now, that's a problem."

"It is? But it's so late. And I'm *so* tired."

"I guess maybe…maybe I could overlook it."

"You're the best." I jumped a little, making the Wonder Twins bounce. "Could I get a room at the back? Bottom floor, please? I just need it for tonight."

"You'll have to pay up front. And there's a twenty-dollar fee for ah, overlooking your lack of ID and credit card."

"No problem." I handed over the cash.

"Room 52." He held out the key, but when I grabbed it he didn't let go. "Why do you need two beds?"

"My girlfriend and I are planning to push them together to make one big bed so we can have a really bouncy naked pillow fight."

His jaw dropped open and his grip went slack. "Ahh…"

I snatched the key from him. Turning back as I left, I gave him a finger wave over my shoulder. "Toodles."

As soon as I got in the car, I burst out laughing. "What is it with guys and naked girl-on-girl pillow fights?"

"If you have to ask you'll never get it," Miguel said. "It's a dude thing."

He drove us around to our room at the back of the hotel and backed into the parking space for a quick getaway.

"I wish I could call Alice," Miguel said as he flipped through one fuzzy channel after another on the TV. So much for the advertised cable TV.

Maybe talking to Alice and hearing her news would light a fire under Miguel to get himself together and start thinking of someone other than himself for a change.

"As long as you use the hotel room phone and make it quick that shouldn't be a problem."

I really needed to check in with Super Agent, but I was afraid he'd do a reverse number look-up or something and be on us faster than the bedbugs I was sure were crawling around on these hideously patterned comforters. I wasn't ready to face him and the repercussions of what I'd done to save Miguel yet.

A few minutes into Miguel's call his face went totally white underneath his week's worth of scruff . *Congratulations*, I mouthed and then pretended to rock an imaginary baby. He glared back at me and turned away, whispering into the receiver.

After a couple more minutes he placed the phone back into its cradle. "You knew about Alice?"

"Yeah. It's one of the reasons I'm here saving your sorry behind. It's bad enough my future niece or nephew has a dumbass for a father. I couldn't let them grow up with a *dead* dumbass for a father."

He dropped his head into his hands and doubled over. "Oh my god. I can't believe this."

"Believe it, Daddy Dumbass."

His head popped up and he fixed me with a look that was a mixture of pissed-off and scared half to death. "Would you quit it with the dumbass remarks? I'm freaking the freak out right now. The least you could do is cut the I-told-you-so's down to about half for a change. I swear sometimes you sound so much like Mom—"

"Don't even put this on me with that sounding-like-Mom B.S. You put your lot in with Sergei, who you knew would cheat you or in some other way or another try to twist things his direction. Then you ran away instead of going to the cops. On top of that you knocked up your girlfriend. And this is all somehow *my* fault?"

"I'm not saying it's your fault. I'm trying to take responsibility here and fix things. The least you can do is try to see it!"

"What I see is a guy who manages to not only screw up his own life but everyone else's he comes in contact with. You want to take responsibility? You want to be the big man? Then don't make dumbass decisions on top of dumbass decisions."

"You're always so critical and judgmental. It wasn't that long ago when you were in deep with Sergei. Talk about throwing your lot in. What do you think that was? Who are you to judge me?"

"That's a low blow even for you."

"But it's the truth. Who's the dumbass now?"

"You still are. By miles. I got out. I got out and turned my life around. You're still doing the same stupid stuff you've done since before you got out of high school. Only now the stakes are higher. You think I want to tell Mom you're dead? Go to your funeral? Or hold Alice's hand while she gives birth to your fatherless child? It's past time you woke up and got a clue, Miguel. Your actions have effects you can't even begin to—"

BAM!

The door crashed open.

"FBI!"

A swarm of agents flooded the room. There was a lot of shouting about hands getting up and bellies on the ground. Next thing I knew I was facedown on the carpet with two of them on top of me. And not in a good way.

More yelling.

I turned my head toward the noise. Miguel was trying to fight them off. *Whack!* They hit him and he went down hard.

"Miguel!" I struggled against their grip and to knock off the guy who was practically sitting on me. "Don't hurt him!"

The agent on top of me hauled me up by the arms, pushed me up against the wall and frisked me. My lipstick, cash and credit card hit the bed.

"Maggie Mae Castro, you're under arrest."

iguel and I were taken to the Sacramento FBI office, shoved in a room and handcuffed to a bench. This wasn't the first time I'd been arrested, but it was the first time I'd ever been arrested by a federal agency. My reward for trying to save my idiot brother. I couldn't wait to see Super Agent's face when he came to bail me out. Only there would be no bailing me out this time. I'd gone too far.

Would he visit me in prison? The conjugal visits would be freakin' *amazing*.

A federal prisoner and a federal agent. That would look really awesome on our wedding invitations. I wondered if they made bride-and-groom cake toppers with the groom in an ill-fitting suit and the bride in an orange jumpsuit. Maybe the wedding planner could work orange into the overall theme.

Oh, who was I kidding? He'd drop me like the career-ender I was. And rightly so.

"What's it like?"

Miguel's quiet question drew me out of my tortured musings. "What?"

"Having a kid?"

"Jesus." He'd caught me off guard with that question. I *never* talked about this. Never. "It hurts like a son of a bitch."

"Yeah, but what's it *like*?"

"How in the hell should I know? I didn't stick around past the hurting-like-hell part. Why are we talking about this *now*?"

"Do you think I'll be a good father? You know…if I ever get out of jail."

"I hope… No, I *think* you'll do the best you can. At least you'd better."

"I'll try. It's going to suck not being there for the birth. For Alice."

"At least you'll be involved however you can. You will, won't you?" At his nod I let out a tense breath. I'd been half afraid Miguel would run from fatherhood just like our dad had. We didn't have the best parental role models. "I'll tell you this… It hurt twice as much doing it alone. Going through everything, making decisions…all of it alone. I didn't want that for Alice. I didn't want your child's mother to go through what I went through."

I lowered my head, trying to hide the sudden tears at the backs of my eyes. "And I didn't want your child growing up with half of what he should have like we did."

"Do you ever think about her?"

"Can we stop talking about this now? This room is likely wired."

"You're probably right." He exhaled a heavy breath. "Thanks."

"What for?"

"For finding me. If you hadn't…"

"I told you to shut up. Don't you ever listen?"

He chuckled. "I love you too."

"Eff off." Then after a moment, because I didn't know if I'd ever get another chance to tell him face to face… "I love you too."

He grinned at me and he looked so much like our father at our age the tears started pricking my eyes again. What the hell was wrong with me today?

The door opened and in walked Super Agent with a couple of the suits who'd burst through our hotel room door. Man, he looked good. And pissed. Reeeaaally pissed.

"Uncuff her," he told one of the agents, hauling a chair over to sit on backwards. "You want to tell me why you didn't follow the plan?" Uh, yeah. Totally pissed. Man, he was hot when angry, all puffed up and stern-faced. Da-yum.

I rubbed at my sore wrists. "There were complications."

He glanced over at Miguel then back at me. "I can only imagine."

"What plan?" Miguel asked.

"You stole a car," Super Agent said, completely ignoring Miguel.

"Sergei put a tracker on the rental and there was no time to procure a new rental. So I improvised."

Miguel piped up again. "What plan? What the heck is going on here?"

"You were supposed to get him and get to the rendezvous point. What happened?"

"I told you, *there was no time.* Sergei was on to your plan so I made a new one."

Super Agent made some kind of hand signal. The other agents freed Miguel from the bench and started to haul him out of the room.

Miguel fixed me with a mistrustful glare, turning to look over his shoulder as they pulled him out the door. "What the heck is going on here, Maggie?"

I only hoped when Miguel heard the full extent of what I'd done for him, he'd forgive me and go along with whatever the FBI wanted. Unfortunately my brother was the kind of guy who would somehow manage to find a way to screw up winning the lottery.

9

*W*hen we were finally alone, Super Agent reached out and traced a finger along my jaw. "Are you all right?"

"I'm fine. I wish your guys hadn't busted down the door when they did. What kind of high-school dropouts is the FBI hiring these days?"

"They thought there might be trouble. They heard yelling."

"That was me giving my idiot brother the lecture he deserved. One of your guys whacked Miguel with a club. Was that totally necessary?"

"I heard he resisted arrest."

"And I heard my boyfriend promise me I wouldn't end up in handcuffs when all this shook out." I held up my hands to show him the marks from the cuffs. "I also heard him say no one would get hurt." I wasn't quite over seeing Miguel get struck by that agent. I could beat the crap out of my brother, but I'd kill anyone who tried to lay a finger on him.

"I'm sorry about that. Since you didn't follow the plan, the agents sent to get you weren't up to speed on who everyone was."

"There were only two of us! We're twins. It's not that hard to figure out."

He looked like he was trying to suppress a laugh. He took a deep breath and let it out. "Like I said, I'm sorry."

"You put a tracker on me, didn't you?" I'd wondered how his FBI guys had found us and a tracker was the only explanation I could come up with. I should've been mad at his nodded confirmation, but I was more curious about how he'd managed it. "How? I ditched everything."

"Your lipstick. You're never without it."

"Well, dang. A girl likes to think she's a *little* bit mysterious."

"Trust me. You're a constant riddle with an ever-changing solution. What did you get from Miguel?"

"It's like I suspected. Sergei took the money."

"And you were going to tell me this when…?"

"When I knew for sure. Miguel managed to get the offshore bank account number. As far as I can tell, Sergei doesn't know he has it."

Super Agent pulled out his cell phone. "Castro has the info we need. A bank account. Yeah. Really? Okay. Thanks." He punched the *End* button on the call. "Miguel's copping to the stolen car. He's saying it was all his idea."

"My brother's an idiot who got in bed with the Russian mob. Not quite the mastermind behind our little escape job." I jabbed my thumb to my chest. "That would be me."

"I'm going to pretend I didn't hear you say that. If Miguel gives us the info we need, he could get total immunity. You would not. So I wouldn't repeat what you just told me."

"Oh." I couldn't help but be surprised that Miguel would take responsibility. Maybe he really was changing. "Got it."

Super Agent leaned back in his chair a little, studying me. I could tell he was working up to something…something he didn't really want to ask, but the FBI Special Agent in him wouldn't let it go. "You were right to tell Miguel the room was wired."

"You heard our whole conversation." Dang it. What was with my lousy luck lately?

He put up a hand. "It's up to you to fill in the blanks when and if you feel like it."

I bent over and scrubbed my hands over my face. There were those darn tears again. He wanted to know about something I didn't dare breathe a word of for fear of the repercussions. "I assume the microphone is still on."

"It's off, but like I said, it's up to you when, how, and if you want to talk about it."

"I know you. You'll just try to dig up the info on your own."

"No, Maggie, I won't. Not on this. I just wanted you to know I heard the conversation. That's all."

"I can't talk about it. Ever. There's too much at stake. If it was just me... I can't. Please try to understand."

"I do."

"Just like that?"

"Just like that."

I stared at him, not quite able to believe it was that simple. Where I came from there was always an agenda, always a knife pressed into your back. But I could see deep in his eyes that it *was* that simple for him. He was giving me his word, and I knew from experience that the man never went back on it.

And maybe that's why after all I'd gone through to keep the secret, I was finally ready to tell it—to him.

"I had a baby that I put up for adoption," I blurted out.

Super Agent's eyes widened for a fraction of a second. He hadn't expected my declaration.

"Sergei's baby."

It didn't feel good to finally get it out. It wasn't a relief. It was the second most terrifying thing I'd ever done in my life. I hadn't talked to anyone about it. Ever. And now that I'd uncorked it, I couldn't stop the flow of words. They gushed out of me faster than I could think about what to say or how to phrase it.

I told him about my friend, Bea, and holding her as she died. I told him about the sheer panic of clutching a positive pregnancy test in my hand after I had finally, *finally* broken free from Sergei and how if he'd found out, he'd never have let me go. I told him about the steps I'd had to take—a fake ID, moving out of state, finding adoptive parents, giving birth alone—just to give my child a better life than anything I could've ever managed to provide.

Then there were the things I didn't have words for, like the constant ache of missing my baby. And how sometimes it would rise up inside of me when I wasn't paying attention and grip me like a fist, stealing my breath.

He must've heard something in my voice or saw something in my face because he suddenly dropped to his knees in front of me and gripped my face in his hands. And that was when I told him about the pictures that arrived every year on her birthday and how I kept them in an envelope in the hidden compartment of my dresser. And how I was terrified everyday that Sergei would somehow find out and what he might do.

I hadn't wanted that life for myself and I sure as heck hadn't wanted it for a child. Every year that passed brought a kind of hesitant relief. I didn't dare fully relax until her eighteenth birthday, and even then I knew I'd never really be free until either Sergei or I was dead.

"Maggie," Super Agent whispered, his breath making my cheeks cold. And that was when I realized I was crying. "I've got you."

I shook my head, wondering why he'd even want me. I was a catastrophe on top of a disaster. Even when I tried to do the right thing I always managed to screw it up. And then he kissed me and every question I had was answered, every doubt soothed away. He loved me. But it wasn't any kind of love I'd ever felt before. It was better and stronger than anything I ever could've imagined.

He eased out of the kiss and smoothed back the strands of hair that stuck to my cheek. "I love you."

"I love you too." I captured his hand in mine and tilted my head into the caress. "What's going to happen to Sergei?"

"Should I be jealous?"

"If you only knew what I had to do to get out. Cutting my arm off would've been less painful. Going back there…to that life…even for a few hours to save Miguel…" I shook my head. "Never again."

"Good." He twisted a ropey length of my hair around his finger. "Because I'm not done with you yet."

"But he's going to jail, right?" I really needed that assurance.

He released the strand and gave me a very direct stare that dared me not to lie to him. "Did he threaten you?"

Sergei didn't have to threaten me. I had more than one reminder on my body of how he'd destroyed my life and what he'd taken from me. Besides his tattoo on my chest, I had an intricate lace of flowered vines across my abdomen that not only spelled out the word "precious" in Greek—if you knew to look for it—it covered the stretch marks from my pregnancy. That tattoo ensured I'd never forget what being with Sergei had cost me.

I shook my head. "Please tell me he's going away."

"If convicted, he could get lengthy jail time and a steep fine."

"How lengthy?"

"Depends on the charges he gets convicted for and the judge. The bigger and broader the swindle the longer the jail term. Judges don't like to see little old ladies bilked out of their life savings."

"What about mob bosses?"

"You mean Kostya?"

I nodded.

"Unless Miguel can give us something on him, he'll

probably walk away from this."

And that would be worse for Sergei than any prison term. My feelings for Sergei were a jumbled mess, but one thing I knew for sure—I didn't wish for anything Kostya would visit upon him.

"What's going to happen to Miguel? You mentioned immunity. Please tell me that means he's not going to prison."

"The U.S. Attorney's office is very anxious to hear what Miguel has to say. Miguel's lawyer should have no problem working out a deal that will likely mean no jail time."

"You're so sexy when you use words like 'deal' and 'no jail time'."

"What about words like 'you're free to go'?"

"Ooh, dang. That's so hot. If this room wasn't such a fishbowl I'd totally mount you like a polo pony."

Laughing his deep, rich chuckle, he stood and held his hand out to me. "Then let's get out of here and make up for lost time."

I put my hand in his and pressed up against him. Fisting the front of his shirt, I hauled him in close. "By the way, Super Agent, I'm not done with you yet either. Not by a long shot."

An excerpt from *Dyed and Gone*
Book One in the Azalea March Mystery Series

Chapter One

It was like being drop-kicked into a Lady Gaga video.

Although I'd never actually *seen* a Lady Gaga video, I was pretty sure the k-k-k-ker-ay-zee I was currently witnessing would measure up.

Techno music pulsed from oversize speakers, competing with the fevered, carnival-barker voice hocking the latest, state-of-the-art revolution in hairstyling. A string of models, looking like refugees from the forest scene in the *Wizard of Oz*, shuffled onto the stage, wearing formfitting bark dresses, their hair wired and twisted to resemble bare tree branches. Lights flashed on the main stage, slicing across the gender-neutral forms posed modern-dance style, their hair geometric origami, symbolizing the effect of time and space on society.

Or some such ridiculousness.

I was in Las Vegas with my best friends, Vivian Moreno and Juan Carlos, to attend the North American Salon Trade Expo, or NAST-E, as Juan Carlos called it. As hairstylists, this event was our Cannes Film Festival. If the festival were held at the overblown Las Vegas convention center and the movies were hairstyling presentations so ludicrous it was like New York Fashion Week had thrown up, then rolled around in the notions department of a craft store.

Juan Carlos and Viv had talked me into coming all the way from Southern California to Vegas, practically twisting my arm the whole way here. They'd insisted that the free casino booze, stroke-inducing lights, and *ching-ching-ching* of the slots were the perfect antidote for what ailed me.

I'd been dangling at the end of a string of very poor romantic choices and losing my grip fast when Vivian had burst into my apartment the day before yesterday. She'd yanked the TV cable right out of the wall, ending my three-day, tear-inducing Hallmark channel marathon.

"Please tell me you haven't bid on any more of those horrible flower dresses," she'd said, hands on hips. This wasn't the first time she'd rescued me from floral disaster.

My guilty gaze flew to the laptop on the coffee table in front of me propped up by a stack of bridal magazines, my finger hovering over the return key. "Ah, no?" Not yet, anyway.

"Azalea!" She rushed over to where I sat on the couch and looked at the screen. "Oh, for God's sake. That's the ugliest one yet." She closed the computer, sat down next to me, and pulled my Buy Now hand into hers. "You can't bury your feelings in sappy movies and vintage Laura Ashley dresses. You're getting out of here. Now. Pack a bag."

How did she always seem to know when I was at my lowest? This particular low had been courtesy of a too-hot-to-be-legal cop who'd done the old I'll-call-you thing and then didn't. The jerk.

Juan Carlos had skidded to a stop in the entryway. He'd leaned on the doorjamb, one hand over his heart, huffing and puffing as though he'd run a marathon instead of up my three front steps. "Please tell me we got here in time to stop Laura Ingles Wilder from adding to her Little House on the Depressed Prairie collection."

"Just," Vivian replied. "You're coming with us," she told me. "You've already booked out the time at the salon for the trip, so no rescheduling appointments. Think of this trip as a cleansing."

True. I *had* marked the time off my busy schedule. All three of us had, which was a feat in itself, as our salon was the busiest in the summer. Still, I wasn't sure I could bring my mood up enough to actually enjoy myself.

"Exactly," Juan Carlos chimed in. "Out with the no good, rotten, no-calling-back bastard and in with free drinks, questionable bets, and mile-high buffet plates."

I thought of the dress I'd been seconds away from buying, with its lace collar, flounced skirt, and two-inch-thick shoulder pads, and I knew they were right. I was at the lowest of lows. Plus, I was pretty sure I already owned that dress in blue.

"Fine," I said, confident with the knowledge that the dress was on my watch list, so if this trip didn't work out, it could still be mine.

So there we were, standing at the back of an audience filled with hairstylists from all over North America and parts of Europe, all watching as Dhane, the sexy signature artist for the hip new Scandinavian hair-product company, Hjálmar, prowled the hair show's main stage. He'd become famous enough in our world to garner a single moniker like Prince or Madonna, and seeing him in person, I could understand why.

Gripping Viv's and Juan Carlos's hands, I tried to suppress the excitement rising up the back of my throat. They'd been right. This was exactly what I needed. We had four whole days ahead of us with nothing to do except immerse ourselves in the latest hair-styling trends and products. For the first time in weeks, I was actually looking forward to something.

"So, when I weave my client's hair, the foils represent the spiritual labyrinth of man's quest to fit into the social mores created by society's inability to intellectualize a person's individual creativity, thereby transferring their reality onto me, the artist. Correct?" Juan Carlos asked with a face straighter than a preelection politician promising lower taxes.

"Uh-huh," Vivian answered absently, standing on tiptoes, trying to see over the crowd, her focus fixed on the black-clad man strutting back and forth across the stage.

Decked out in her usual black and white with a red flower pinned in her hair, Vivian looked like a Mexican Betty Boop, all petite curves and what-of-it? attitude. I could never match her attitude, but I had almost as many curves as her. Even though she was a few inches shorter than me and a few shades tanner, we were often mistaken for sisters, which I thought was more due to our closeness than our resemblance. Other than both of us having dark hair, we looked nothing alike. Even though I could only hope for cheekbones like hers, I consoled myself with the fact that my lips were fuller.

"And if I buy their DVD with the bonus, one of a kind, life-altering weaving combs, I'll be taking back my power as an artist. Is that right?" Juan Carlos inquired further.

I clapped a hand over my mouth, trapping the laughter. This was going to be the *best* weekend ever.

"Yes. Yes." Viv waved him quiet. Putting a finger to her deep red lips, she emphasized her point. "Ssh!"

"I see." Juan Carlos stroked his clean-shaven chin as if giving this philosophy great thought. He was trying a new look, very *Mad Men*, with his dark, shiny hair parted and combed to the side and a vintage, man-about-home cardigan sweater with a collared shirt and slim-fit slacks.

The crowd of hairstylists around us watched, enthralled, as more tree people sprang up from the stage like, well, trees, and Dhane, now on bended knee, wound up his pitch to convert every stylist in the room to the Hjálmar, eco-friendly way of doing hair.

"Oh, Mother Earth, forgive us." Lightning cracked on the screen behind him. The expected thunder shook the floor, making my feet tingle, my exhilaration rising to a new level. "We've killed your trees, your plants, your animals." Images of dead animal carcasses as big as Volkswagens appeared on the screen behind Dhane. "We've desecrated your oceans and streams." Now they showed sea creatures, birds, fish, and other aquatic wildlife, dead or covered in oil. "Please, forgive us." His laser-blue eyes bore down on the crowd from the three Jumbotrons high above the stage, clearly gearing up for the big finale. "We've studied. We've learned. We give you...Hjálmar!"

The stage plunged into darkness, the only light coming from the giant *H* of the Hjálmar logo intertwined with healthy, living plants and wildlife on all four screens. The crowd surged to its feet, the applause, whistles, and shouts loud enough to drop fowl from the air. The house lights came up. I guessed there wouldn't be an encore. Not that he needed one.

An announcement came over the loud speakers, a sexy female voice with a Swedish accent. "Thank you for sharing the Hjálmar vision. Dhane will be presenting the Stylist of the Year Award at the North American Styling Awards sponsored by Hjálmar."

The North American Styling Awards, or NASA, was the most prestigious beauty competition in North America and was considered the hair-styling equivalent of winning an Oscar. As last year's winner, Dhane would naturally present the award to this year's top stylist.

We made our way, herdlike, out onto the main floor of the convention center. Row upon row of manufacturer booths gridded the room, each one promoting the most high-tech, necessary styling tools, products, and equipment a salon or hairstylist would ever want.

Juan Carlos was the first to break our stunned silence. "Holy TV evangelist! I've got the strongest urge to repent. I feel like I've been to church. I'll bet I'm healed. Oh my God! I can't feel my bunions anymore, and my shoes fit better." He examined his hands as we walked. "Ah, darn, I still have that nick on my middle finger from when I was cutting my client Courtney's hair, and she jumped up to chase after her sleazo boyfriend who walked past the salon with another girl." He showed me his cut finger.

"Bummer. Did she catch him?"

"She did." He rubbed the cut. "It was worth it. I got a new client out of it."

"How?"

"The other girl had the nastiest hair so I took pity on her and booked her the following week."

I gave him a look and shook my head.

"What?"

"I want to check out the Hjálmar booth. Come on." Vivian grabbed my sleeve. I grabbed Juan Carlos's sleeve, creating a chain. Vivian towed us toward the center of the grid, where the big names in hair-care products like Paul Mitchell, Wella, and Sebastian had booths.

The Hjálmar booth was at the center, a choice spot, and was set up like a cosmetics counter in a department store. It was oval in shape and about as long as a double-car garage. The guys and gals behind the counter pranced and posed with the put-out pouts of Abercrombie and Fitch models.

Huge posters hung above the racks of product in the center, featuring more emaciated, disenfranchised youths leaping through meadows, holding various Hjálmar products, their clothing fluttering in the breeze. But these posters were nothing compared to the much larger ones of Hjálmar's star stylist, Dhane. His vivid blue eyes stared down at us from on high as if surveying his kingdom. His gaze was mesmerizing. Looking too long at him made me kind of dizzy.

"Is it me, or do the center of his eyes spin like a pinwheel?" I asked.

"Azalea," Juan Carlos whispered, hitting me in the arm to get my attention, repeatedly, annoyingly.

"What?" I barked, turning to see what he was so wound up about.

Juan Carlos's attention was fixed on the figure headed our way, parting the crowd like Moses.

Dhane strode purposefully as a captain would to the helm of his ship. He was flanked by suits who I assumed were Hjálmar executives, his pale shoulder-length hair rippling behind him. Seeing him up close was nothing like seeing him onstage or in a picture. I'd thought he was attractive. I was wrong.

He was stunning. Beautiful. But it was the careful, fragile beauty of a delicate orchid, easily marred or crushed.

Juan Carlos made a sound like a balloon losing air. I knew the feeling. If I'd been capable of more than staring gawk-eyed and gape-mouthed, I might've thrown myself at Dhane's feet.

Dhane spotted us and made a slight change of direction, heading our way. Juan Carlos hit my arm again, like I hadn't been watching every move Dhane made. Vivian shifted her stance, putting out a hip, and patted her hair. What in the what? I glanced back and forth between Vivian and Dhane, my brows bunching tighter together with every step he took. Did they know each other?

Dhane reached us and my first thought was that he was taller than I'd imagined he'd be. My next thought was thoroughly naughty and completely unrepeatable.

He grasped Vivian's hands, kissing both in turn. "My Vivian." His accent was much more pronounced in person, sounding vaguely European and kind of forced, as though he'd practiced to get it just right. "I'd know you anywhere."

"It's been a long time." Vivian smiled, batting her eyelashes at him.

My brows bounced up and I stared in openmouthed astonishment. Vivian *did* know Dhane. From where? When? How? And why in the hell didn't I know about this?

"And yet you look the same. How is this possible?"

Vivian giggled. Giggled! Viv didn't do smitten teenager. Not even when she had been a teenager. Um, hello! *Somebody* was forgetting all about her boyfriend of three years back home.

Juan Carlos nudged me out of the way, hinting at an introduction. But it was as if Dhane and Vivian were alone in the room, their gazes so entwined not even Juan Carlos's throat clearing and posturing could break their bond. It took a sharp nudge in the shoulder from Juan Carlos for Viv to return to us.

"Oh, sorry. Dhane, I'd like you to meet my friends. This is Juan Carlos. He's a stylist at my salon and a dear friend."

Dhane kept ahold of Vivian's hand while extending his other to shake Juan Carlos's. "Pleasure to meet you."

"Mine, too," Juan Carlos purred.

"And this is Azalea, my best friend and business partner."

Dhane turned his brilliant blues on me. Were it not for the hand he'd clasped, I'd have swooned like a lovesick boy-band fan. "Azalea, so nice to meet you at last."

At last? I looked a question at Vivian. Boy did my best friend have a lot of explaining to do.

"How long are you in town?" Vivian recaptured Dhane's attention, leaving Juan Carlos and me to exchange looks of confusion and conjecture.

"I am to stay for the awards and then return to Europe for another event." They were in the vortex again, just the two of them. "Will you meet me later?"

"Of course."

Dhane smiled, and I could have sworn a choir of angels sang. "We have much to discuss, no?"

One of the executives tugged Dhane's sleeve. "She's waiting. We have to go."

Dhane cast him an annoyed look mixed with something else—fear, maybe?

"A moment," he told them, then turned back to Vivian.

"I am looking forward to spending time with you." They exchanged cell phone numbers and a lingering good-bye.

Vivian, Juan Carlos, and I stood shoulder to shoulder, watching Dhane leave. The crowd that had gathered made room for his departure, surreptitiously casting furtive glances at him in that way you do with celebrities when you recognize them but don't want to pester them. A few gave Vivian curious looks, no doubt wondering if she was someone they should recognize. A few others didn't bother to hide their jealousy before they turned their backs and followed Dhane.

I shoved Vivian's shoulder. "Why did I not know that you knew Dhane?"

Juan Carlos joined in. "I cannot believe it! I should shun you. This is unforgivable...but I might consider forgiveness if you tell all. And I do mean *all*."

Vivian spun away, leaving us to scramble after her.

"Come on, Viv. How'd you meet him? How long have you known him?" I would have continued peppering her with questions, but she stopped me with a, "Ssh" and a, "Not here."

Juan Carlos and I followed her out into a hallway and down a corridor to a small, out of the way windowed alcove with a view of the famous Las Vegas strip.

"Okay, you can't repeat what I'm about to tell you, got it?" She seemed nervous, casting furtive glances around as though she were about to give up state secrets or something.

Juan Carlos and I bobbed our heads. In that moment, we would have traded our finely honed, ridiculously expensive hair-cutting shears to hear what she had to say.

"All right." She cast a wary eye around us, making sure she wouldn't be overheard. "I met Dhane when I was sixteen during the summer I went to stay with my aunt Tita in Wichita."

So just before Vivian and I had met in beauty school. I

felt a little pang of jealousy at the thought that Dhane had known her longer than I did.

"She'd just had twins and my mom sent me to help her, since all of our family is in California." Vivian paused. "I really shouldn't be telling you this. I promised."

"We won't tell. We swear." I glanced at Juan Carlos to get his agreement.

"Absolutely," Juan Carlos agreed. "Even if you dipped me in hot oil and pulled my fingernails out one by one. Or did that water-torture thing with the drips on the forehead, my lips would stay sealed. Cross my heart, hope to die—"

Vivian stopped him with a hand. "Got it. You won't tell." She took a deep breath and another look around. "Aunt Tita had put the babies down for a nap, so I had some free time. I decided to go for a walk."

She stopped again and looked out the window, but her gaze was unfocused, as if she were looking more within than without. I got the impression that she'd buried this part of her past so deep for so long that it took a great deal of effort for her to pry it loose.

After a moment, she continued, "I was walking, not really paying much attention to what I was doing. I was just so glad to be out of the house. It was hot, really hot. I put a hand up to wipe the sweat off my forehead and that's when I got grabbed from behind and pulled into a space between two apartment buildings."

She turned and paced a couple of steps away, then back again. "I was scared out of my mind. I thought he'd kill me. He told me to give him my watch and the pearl earrings I got from my grandma for my fourteenth birthday. He was big, huge. Like I said, I was really afraid. But my grandma had given me those earrings right before she died. I couldn't just hand them over."

She crossed her arms tightly over her chest, hugging herself. "He hit me. I went down and stayed down. I figured if he thought I was dead, he'd leave me alone." She rubbed her arms. "But he didn't. He bent down over me. I held my breath and tried to be as still as possible. And then he was on top of me. I panicked and screamed, kicking and hitting at him, but he was just too heavy."

"Oh, Viv." I took a step toward her, but she waved me off.

"I'm fine. I was fine because of Dhane. Only his name wasn't Dhane then."

Juan Carlos's eyes bugged out of his head. "What...what happened? Go back. What happened with the guy?"

"He was heavy because he'd been hit in the head with a brick. Dhane hit him. He saved me." I could tell her emotions were right there at the surface, reflecting in her dark brown eyes.

"Then what?" I asked, knowing there had to be more, a lot more.

"Dhane was skinny then, you know, in that young kid, gangly kind of way. But he was really cute even then." She cracked a hint of that secretive smile I was already beginning to associate with Dhane. "He helped me up and then he handed me my watch back, but not before he'd kicked the guy in the gut." She laughed. "I think I fell for him right then."

"You and Dhane?" Juan Carlos asked with more than a hint of awe and an obvious twinge of envy.

"Well, no. I was a good Catholic girl. But we did fool around a bit." She looked off, that grin playing around her mouth again. "I sneaked out as often as I could to see him. And then the summer was over and I had to go back home."

"Did you see him again?" I asked.

"Yes, a few more times. Another summer and then he came out to see me. By then I was in beauty school and we were just friends. I showed him a little of what I was learning. He picked it up quickly. He had a natural talent for working with hair."

"You said that his name wasn't Dhane then," Juan Carlos reminded her.

She looked confused. "I did?"

We nodded.

"Oh, well, I guess he wanted a new identity, a new name. His home life wasn't the greatest and he wanted to distance himself from it. He came up with the name Dhane and I thought it fit."

"Wow, you helped create Dhane." Juan Carlos said this as if Vivian had invented a flying car or something.

"No, Dhane created Dhane. He worked really hard and he deserves his success."

"What was his real name?" I asked.

She shook her head, scanning the small alcove as if she'd already said too much. "That's for Dhane to tell."

"If he's from Kansas, then how'd he get the accent?" Juan Carlos asked.

"It was part of reinventing himself." She bit her lip, and her voice took on a pleading, desperate tone. "Look, please don't say anything to anybody. This is important. Please promise me you'll keep what I'm telling you to yourself."

She'd told us everything she was going to, and I got the impression she regretted even that small amount. I examined Vivian's face in that way we did when we wanted to know what the other is thinking. She avoided meeting my eyes.

I knew Vivian better than I knew myself. There was something else going on here. And as soon as I could get her alone, I was going to find out just what that was. The one thing I knew for sure was that Vivian seemed very protective of Dhane, and keeping his secret was extremely important to her. Being the keeper of more than a few of my secrets, I knew Viv would never spill Dhane's.

I also knew without a doubt that the story she'd told us was at best incomplete and at worst a total and complete lie.

Giving her my word of honor to keep what she'd told us to myself, I couldn't help but wonder what she'd left out…and why.

About the Author

Award-winning author **Beth Yarnall** writes mysteries, romantic suspense and the occasional hilarious blog post. A storyteller since her playground days, Beth remembers her friends asking her to make up stories of how the person "died" in the slumber-party game *Light as a Feather, Stiff as a Board*, so it's little wonder she prefers writing stories in which people meet unfortunate ends. In middle school, she discovered romance novels, which inspired her to write a spoof of soap operas for the school's newspaper. She hasn't stopped writing since.

For a number of years, Beth made her living as a hairstylist and makeup artist and at one time owned a salon. Somehow, hairstylists and salons always seem to find their way into her stories. Beth lives in Southern California with her husband, two sons and their rescue dog where she is hard at work on her next novel.

For more information about Beth and her novels please visit her website or join her newsletter at:
www.bethyarnall.com.

You can also visit with Beth on
Facebook: http://www.facebook.com/BethYarnallAuthor
Twitter: http://www.twitter.com/BethYarnall